COVER

STORIES

COVER

STORIES

EDITED BY STEFAN KIESBYE

VOLTBOOKS

Sonoma State University
Rohnert Park, CA 94928
www.volt-books.com

Book design by Don Mitchell
Cover design by Cal Blick

ISBN 978-0-9988072-0-1
Library of Congress Control Number: 2017903981

"Tricoter" was first published in *Ninth Letter*, 2007.
"Of the Revolution" first appeared in the *New England Review*,
2012.
"When the Saints Come" was published in the collection *Ex-Yu*
(Véhicule Press, 2015).
"Possibly Forty Ships" was published in the collection *Crushed
Mexican Spiders* (Unbound, 2012).

Contents

Introduction   7

Derek Nikitas —The Call   11
Jessica Anthony —Dear Stranger   51
Jason Ockert —Mrs. Hutchinson's Bones   59
Brian Evenson —The Other Neighbors   73
Joe Oestreich —Tricoter   83
Stefan Kiesbye —To Build a Fire   93
Stacy Bierlein —Wants   101
Jane Dykema —Luna Beach   107
Alexander Lumans —Craigslist Missed Connections   125
Brock Clarke —Of the Revolution   141
Terese Svoboda —Murderinging The Dead Father   151
Jeff Parker —The Penis   157
Jane Ridgeway —Peredelkino   177
Tibor Fischer —Possibly Forty Ships   187
Paul Elwork —Shame the Devil   201
Josip Novakovich —When the Saints Come   215

The Contributors   241
Original Stories   247
Acknowledgments   249

INTRODUCTION

STEFAN KIESBYE

When I first heard "Tainted Love," I was fourteen and lived in a small northern town in Germany. Only weeks or months later did I find out that Soft Cell's hit was not the first version of the song. Neither was Kim Carnes' "Bette Davis Eyes," or Bryan Ferry's "Jealous Guy." Yet to me they were, and have stayed, the ones that mattered and that I can't get out of my head. They were originals. To this day, when I hum "Little Drummer Boy," I eventually add David Bowie's line, "Peace on Earth."

In 2015, a friend wrote, "I know what it sounds like, what I would think if you told me that. But listen." She was talking about Ryan Adams' version of Taylor Swift's album *1989*. That was the start of this book.

From our parents we learn how to use forks and knives, but we ask books the darker questions we have. They are abrasive friends, friends that kick and scratch and bite and force us to think past what we expected and wished for. We also realize that every story leaves a multitude of stories untold. Whatever happened to the ferryman in the Brothers' Grimm "The Devil With the Three Golden Hairs"? What happened to Red Schuhart after finding the Golden Sphere?

What did the woman in the dunes think about Niki Jumpei that first evening down in her house? How would Lady Brett Ashley have written about the fiesta?

In literature covers abound though no one calls them that. Our work answers the stories we've read. What we add to what already exists is the part we call creative. Bertolt Brecht's *Threepenny Opera*, Jane Smiley's *A Thousand Acres*, and Jean Rhys' *Wide Sargasso Sea*, pick up already-told stories again, spin them further, alter or reinterpret the material. The lyrics change, but the themes can still be heard.

I asked the writers in this anthology to choose a story they loved and write a cover. There the guidelines ended. You'll find no line-by-line recreation of Don Quixote. Instead you will rediscover the Iliad, Ivan Ilyich, a tell-tale heart, Mrs. Hutchinson's prolonged death, and the further adventures of Jim and Harriet Stone. You'll meet the dead father and Cthulhu again. Every story's starting point lies within another writer's work, another writer's invention. The results are entirely original.

THE CALL

DEREK NIKITAS

I. THE HARUSPEX

ALL I EVER WANTED was to *know*.

I have made a profession of deciphering secrets. I have tilted Babylonian tablet against the light to read history in the wedges pressed like tooth-marks across the clay. Once there were men like me who sought the stars for answers, contemplated dreams, read fortunes in sacrificial blood—all of us desperate to be called up for enlightenment....

This story begins in 1986 with the death of my son Scott. He was only nineteen, a sophomore at the Rhode Island School of Art and Design, on the day the police called me to his Fox Point apartment, just a few blocks from my own in College Hill. All these years later I still remember what I noticed first as I climbed the cramped spiral staircase to his floor: deep scrape marks freshly gouged into the wood steps.

Then, already dizzy from the climb, I smelled sulfur and collapsed in the doorway at the sight of what awaited me just over the threshold: blood spilled across the floor, severed organs in ritual arrangement....

I sometimes think maybe a spark of *self* passes down to one's child, so that even when he matures into his total otherness, one feels that magnetic pull to be whole with him again, and if he dies, one is lost, drifting toward nothing forever....

Or rather, this story doesn't truly start in 1986, but much later, in the new millennium. By that time I'd been in a stupor of fifteen years since Scott's death—*alive*, yes, teaching my courses and directing dissertations in the Department of Egyptology and Assyriology at Brown, but much like the zombie in the thought experiment, I was a shell of myself.

Yes, when I consider the full confluence of events, I can say for certain that this story starts one September afternoon on a train from Providence to Penn Station, where I sat with my forehead pressed against the window glass and my attention directed fifty feet down into a river bed. In this moment, I *awoke*.

I clutched the armrest and held my breath against the swaying of the passenger car, but my heart wouldn't settle even after we'd crossed the bridge. I was on this train headed to the City because I had to confront someone. I had to track down a stranger who was exploiting my son's death, and I was terrified as a soldier in a trench.

Who was the stranger? I didn't yet know. Under the webmaster alias "Son-Web," this individual operated a site called *halleysconflict.com*, a dumping ground of digitized news clips, testimonials, dream logs, and other muddled minutiae concerning the 1986 Halley's Comet "fly-by."

All of this research was somehow meant to prove the comet's proximity had induced a few weeks of faintly detectable global hysteria noticed only by a select few sensitive types—Scott being one of them, at least according to the site.

This *Son-Web* person's delusions would've escaped my notice, except that a colleague from Physics alerted me to Scott's virtual presence on the *halleysconflict* site, and the terrible misinformation provided about his death. Worst of all, this webmaster had somehow appropriated *and posted* crime scene photographs leaked from the Providence Police Department. All this, because Scott died on April 11th, the date Halley's Comet flew closest to Earth, and *Son-Web* believed there to be some cosmic implication involved.

I'm no hothead, but something about the affront, the invasion of such tender private affairs, made me so livid I wanted to reproach this *Son-Web* in person. His online bio placed him in Brooklyn, so I had hired an ex-NYPD investigator named Raymond Legrasse to track him down. Only when I was en route did I begin to doubt my convictions, not to mention my imaginary construct of *Son-Web* as a bookish shut-in easily intimidated by another like himself. I considered it might've been less taxing just to send a terse email.

Then, just as I stepped off the train in Manhattan, a brute in a baseball cap lunged out from the mob of commuters on the platform and snatched my arm. I was too shocked to cry out—a relief, because he turned out to be Detective Legrasse, the man I had hired.

"Situation's changed, Professor Angell," he said, offering me a wallet-sized high school photo of an African-American teenager. She was scowling at the camera.

"Her name's Sonia Webb," he said, nodding at the photo.

Fifteen, currently living with a foster family in Red Hook.

"We'll have to handle this some other way," Legrasse told me. "Like maybe a cease-and-desist, because I can't have you harassing some kid."

He was right, of course—not just about her age, but her race, her sex, her class. In this power dynamic, I was the perfect emblem of oppression. To go anywhere near her would be monstrous.

And yet my Scott—those photos she'd posted of his lifeless body, where anyone could find them, even children. To this girl, Scott was an urban legend in black-and-white. She never knew his heart, his personal struggles. I just wanted her to realize.

Legrasse thrust out his barrel chest and ordered me onto the next train back to Providence, as if he still had legal authority in this district. It was better not to argue, better to nod meekly and mutter about a nearby bookstore I wanted to visit before I headed back home.

An hour later I was alone among the graffitied brick warehouses and chain-link fences of Red Hook, exhausted after just a few blocks' walk in oppressive heat. I had to hold up my glasses to keep them from slipping off my nose.

Sonia Webb's housing project looked more like a prison complex than a residence, complete with delinquents lifting weights in the exercise yard. In my blazer and slacks I had no chance of slipping past unnoticed.

I wanted to turn back, but Scott compelled me once again. Once, I could've saved him, if only I'd had the strength to push back against his addictions and his mania. All I had left now was to do him justice.

The building felt alive with music thumping and rumbling across the walls, scattered voices raised in distress. Nobody stopped my entering, but then nobody answered Sonia's apartment door, either. My nerves were on edge. My presence clearly agitated the young men loitering in the hall. Against all logic, I expected Legrasse to step around a corner and arrest me for stalking an underage girl.

I'd had enough. Hurrying back downstairs, I nearly collided with a furtive figure headed upward—a burst of pajama pants and beaded braids. Her scowl I recognized straight away.

Sonia froze in the stairwell, clutching her backpack straps.

"Miss Webb, I'm Dr. George Angell...." I began.

In a flash, her combat boots were bashing up the concrete steps again. I considered chasing after her, but now that her existence was so much more palpable, I couldn't think what I'd say. So I left. Outside, the sun pierced my eyes like a cosmic accusation: *You have failed your son.*

I retreated past a dockyard full of screeching seagulls, dabbing at my neck with a handkerchief. My scalp burned and all my regrets clawed at each other for prominence.

Then a voice, behind me, "Yo, professor." Sonia Webb.

We took a booth in a fast food place, though the girl could barely stay seated. She sat on her legs and tugged at her braids and twisted her drink straw into knots. The bags under her eyes were much too heavy for a child her age. She spoke too fast in that muddled urban manner—and in a conspiratorial whisper, no less, her eyes darting at every entering customer.

It seemed my surprise appearance in the stairwell had startled her, but a few minutes locked in her apartment made her realize I might have *valuable information*, as she put it. From the pockets of her backpack she produced notebooks and folders and spread them over the greasy tabletop, as if I was there to assess her work, to *contribute*.

"So who was it sent you?" she asked.

"I don't know what you mean. My son, Scott—"

"You know what I'm saying, Professor. Like a secret club. Illuminati-type shit. Don't try and tell me you ain't all connected like that."

Without even waiting for an answer, she launched into a monologue. Her intention was to draw lines of causality between Halley's Comet and adverse world events surrounding April 1986, including a bombing in Berlin, a downpour of hailstones that killed a hundred Bangladeshis, Chernobyl. On the very day Scott died there was an FBI shootout in Miami. The Challenger disaster prefigured these events by three months, she said, "and they were supposed to jet up there to study the comet. Did you know that?"

She opened a notebook to reveal her dream journal, citing various entries as evidence—of *what*, I couldn't ascertain. That for the last few months she'd been cursed with constant night terrors? She'd sketched sand pits in the desert, meteors burning through the atmosphere, towers billowing smoke, dead horses washing ashore....

Amphetamines were a possibility, but her manner was too sharp, too focused. Instead I suspected a mood disorder, paranoid fantasies, echoes of what had plagued my son. I couldn't shake her resemblance to him, lurking just below the obvious differences between them.

"You're a bright young woman," I told her.

"For a Negro hood rat, you mean. How'd I even tackle html, right? I'm smart enough to spot condescending, *Pro-fess-or*. Listen, there's people all over contacting my website with these same problems, these same *things* coming up in their nightmares. You watch, something's gonna go down."

A week before his death, Scott stormed into my apartment and demanded that I decode a cuneiform script he'd penciled onto a sketch pad. It was, after all, my line of work. When Scott was younger we'd press a chopstick stylus into Play-Doh to form secret messages in the Ugaritic cuneiform alphabet—but what he'd drawn was nothing like that. It looked like an unstudied mock-up of more ancient Babylonian pictographs, a prank.

After much gnashing of teeth, he admitted he copied it from a persistent dream, etchings he'd seen on the rounded inner walls of an imagined tower. But his dreams had become constant, urgent. That night I was too stunned by his behavior to help him—not with the script, but with his mental state. I felt like I'd ruined him irrevocably, like I'd failed my watch.

Fifteen years later, I saw that same obsession infecting this young woman—as if Scott's fantasies had carried on through the gossip of his friends and spread outward to conspiracy theorists like Sonia. It was too much to bear, far too much.

Without warning, she grabbed my wrist. She had an electric current all her own, an intensified life coursing through her, into me. Everything I knew about Scott's final days, anything he might've told me about his visions—she wanted to know all of it. Did I save any of his sculptures? *Anything.*

I hadn't yet told her I was there to make her stop.

"Okay, all right," she said. "Let's talk about your jam."

"My—?"

"Your area of expertise. *Divination.*"

After a calming breath I explained that my area was Bronze Age Mesopotamian history and culture—that my interest in bārû, the diviner priests who read the future through *extispicy*, was purely academic.

"Extra spicy? What now?" She hitched her eyebrows.

"I have a feeling you know full well. It's prophecy through the examination of the vital organs of a sacrificed animal, in particular the liver."

"What ever happened to fortune cookies, right?"

"I don't actually *believe* in it, Sonia. To be clear."

"But, still—think about it. You poke through all those broken up tablets, looking for shards of info. You puzzle it all together. You decipher. It's all the same game, professor."

She was sharper than most of my ivy league undergrads. I shut my eyes and remembered the carnage on Scott's apartment floor, the two uniformed officers crouched over my body when I woke from my initial fainting spell. *Sorry we didn't warn you, Dr. Angell. No worries, though. It's only a sheep.*

No worries. The blood wasn't Scott's, but my only child had still taken his own life by hanging.

The story quickly emerged: before his suicide, he'd led a live sheep into his apartment house and up the spiral stairs, its unsteady hooves gouging the steps. He'd said a prayer to Hadad, perhaps, then gutted the animal and removed its organs. He couldn't have known what to look for. It was merely a gruesome pantomime of an ancient practice—a final act meant to shock the loved ones he left behind. A punishment for neglect.

Those were the years of *satanic panic.* Scott wore his hair like the heavy metal rockers in the posters decked all around his room. Everywhere, demonic faces with tongues lolling out. Steel-plated skeletons. Thus, the investigators reached their own conclusions about the nature of Scott's ritual suicide.

Sonia knew all this, of course. Her website offered police photos of the mutilated sheep, as if some modern-day haruspex who stumbled upon her site might divine, so many years later, the revelations that drove my son to kill himself.

"Please understand," I begged her. "Scott was mentally ill."

Undaunted, Sonia urged more papers into my hand, Xeroxed newspaper reports from April 11th, the date of my son's death and Halley's closest proximity to Earth. In a Mississippi junkyard, a suspected occult murder and disembowelment. Reports of child abuse at a Milwaukee daycare center. An attempted Vancouver kidnapping, the culprit claiming amnesia and temporary insanity. A riot at a rock concert. A mesmerizing barrage of supposed evidence that seemed to coalesce and then just as quickly dissolve.

"My God," I realized aloud. "The day Scott died. It was your birthday, wasn't it?"

The epiphany set my heart off its rhythm. When I pressed my hand to my chest, Sonia said, "You can feel it, can't you? Like an electric storm, or like a pager vibration, all across your body. A call that makes no noise. I been talking to people all over the city. We're *hearing* it."

Back in Providence that night I lay sleepless in bed, fretting about Sonia and her psychological well-being. The girl had become a lightning rod for my most anxious thoughts. Still, I had to be vigilant against conflating my concern with her delusions. It would've been so easy to convince myself I could've saved Scott—or helped Sonia—if only I indulged their obsessions.

When I shut my eyes I saw no visions, only darkness.

For the first time in years I opened the box of Scott's personal effects. Among the Polaroids and anatomy sketches, the loose keys and foreign coins he'd collected, was a yellow legal pad marked up with mostly illegible notes. And that page of cuneiform script he'd copied from his dreams.

Time had dulled the graphite wedges, but I could still read it well enough to be sure it was nonsense. He'd been so convinced, so desperate for me to make meaning out of it. Now, nothing he'd left behind hollowed my soul more than that script.

Naturally, the police had poured over these materials before they turned them over to me. They suspected Scott's involvement in a satanic cult of animal abusers, but having no proof that such a group existed, they eventually dropped the issue.

No suicide note, no motive, a clean toxicology report.

Restless, I examined his legal pad with an attentiveness I could never muster before. It was Sonia's influence on me.

The notes were reading logs from various texts mostly known to me. Cotton Mather, Madame Blavatsky, biblical Apocrypha....

The one text I didn't know was *Al Azif* (meaning in Arabic "the whistling wind" or perhaps "the insect buzz"). Scott's notes from the book outlined a number of natural disasters and other unexplained phenomena in the ancient world— floods, droughts, lunar cycles, and several possible references to earlier visits from Halley's Comet.

Later, my research would reveal that *Al Azif* was a compendium of occult knowledge concerning these natural phenomenon, not to mention a grimoire of incantations for evoking assorted djinn, purportedly written by a third-century Arab mystic named Abdallah Zahr-ad-din and printed only once in English, by a London press, in 1895.

The only copy publicly available in the United States—the only copy Scott could've consulted—was housed in Special Collections at the Orne Library of Miskatonic University in Arkham, Massachusetts.

The following Saturday I rode the bus to Arkham and presented myself to the reference librarian, whose agitation manifested the instant I asked her for the book. My credentials gave me no help. She snorted out a caustic laugh and asked how it was I didn't already know *Al Azif* has been stolen from their collection five months earlier.

The thief, described by witnesses as a young African-American female, had used a stolen student ID card to gain access to the book, peeled the security tape from inside the spine, and then simply slipped out of the library.

That night I called the phone number Sonia had given me, but there was no answer. I recall the date distinctly because early the next morning, our department secretary blustered into my Ancient Mesopotamia course with urgent news that sent all my students rushing out of the lecture hall.

We had been attacked.

I called Sonia three more times throughout the day, while the television replayed its footage of the falling towers, while the news anchors babbled. She lived so close to the epicenter. Soon the power grids would go dark, whole branches of government would collapse—I felt sure of it.

Just as Sonia had *felt* this would happen.

But at nightfall civilization still marched on, and I hadn't eaten all day. At the neighborhood market, a beef liver sat on display behind the meat counter. I stared into the dark grooves of the lobus sinister—*the naplastum*—the renal and colic impressions, the *land* and *median* and *palace* of the caudate lobe... and wondered what dark prophecy a bārû might divine from it all.

"Can I help you, sir?" the butcher asked.

I was the only pedestrian on Benefit Street. The lamps gave majesty to the colonial facades and the white bell tower of the First Unitarian Church, but the world felt passed on, deserted.

My apartment stairwell light was on the fritz, so I tapped blindly at the door lock with what I hoped was the right key. A shift in the air made me catch my breath. A shuddering voice, a hand brushing my elbow, and I leaped into the foyer like a squirrel from a branch.

Sonia was much too charged to notice how badly she'd startled me. She let herself into the apartment and paced the floorboards, listing the imminent signs she'd missed, lamenting how easily she might've predicted the attacks, if only....

What a relief to see her safe, but not here in my private home, unsupervised. I could only imagine what the police might think if they found her alone here with me. She swatted away all my nagging questions and concerns until I asked about *Al Azif*.

At that, she tossed her backpack onto my armchair and lifted out the contraband book. "Did you know," she asked me, "the dude who wrote this book, Abdallah Zahr-ad-din, he was a mystic, right? And he had this following, like a cult, for *centuries*. I mean, his successors did. This shit beats Islam by like two hundred years, but when the Ottomans showed up and started lopping off heads with their scimitars, a bunch of these cultists split the desert to settle way across the world in Little Syria. You know what that was? A used-to-be-happening hood north of Battery Park, until it stalled out and got knocked down to make room for...."

"...the World Trade Center," I realized.

"*Now* you see it!" She slapped her palm atop the book.

What I saw was a series of disconcerting coincidences, random snags in the fabric of history and reality. I did not see a cohesive narrative.

My worries were far more immediate, though eventually, after Sonia insisted her foster parents cared little for her whereabouts, I stopped peering through the curtains for police lights.

We drank tea and talked until dawn. I broached the subject of her mental health, but Sonia would only grumble about mandated counseling and the pills she refused to take because they clouded her thoughts. She judged the existence of her birth parents to be an unfounded rumor, and I wondered if these myths she'd built around her birth date were a coping mechanism.

The hidden workings of the universe to which only supple minds like Scott and Sonia herself were attuned....

When she boarded a bus back to New York, I gave her two hundred dollars and Scott's notes and sketches, even the cuneiform dream-script. She was eager for life, and I didn't care anymore that her theories were fiction. My doubt was a lifeless thing compared to her faith. I'd helped her where I'd forsaken Scott, and that was what mattered most.

Of course I considered adopting her, but within two years she was graduated from high school and accepted at Brown with a scholarship. She lived in the dorms but visited me often, even as new friendships divided some of her attention, and rightly so.

It was Christmas break her sophomore year when she came through my door alight with nervous energy. I had acted out this scene before and would not fail a second time.

Her old website was defunct by then, but she'd long been *gathering research* through more obscure online channels. There was something stirring in Indonesia, she said. People she needed to speak to, sites she had to visit immediately.

I didn't pretend to understand. Instead, I funded her plane ticket and the rest of her travel expenses with no questions asked. All I wanted was an email check-in every other day.

She wrote me daily from internet cafes in Jakarta, then later in outlying Sumatra—block paragraphs about dark energies and vivid dreams, about spiraling ever nearer to the core, but never any concrete detail concerning her travels or discoveries. To avoid my own nervous breakdown, I ignored the constant alarms in my conscience.

The day after Christmas, the tsunami washed over Sumatra.

Afterward there were no more emails.

II THE TRAIL OF DETECTIVE LAGASSE

I SUFFERED NIGHTMARES, yes, but never the kind that prophesied disaster, never those Yeatsian visions, slouching across the desert....

Instead my nightmares offered death—Scott's last choking panic as the rope squeezed tight, legs kicking at the empty air. Or Sonia pressed by tons of rushing water against a concrete barrier, water rising, filling her ears and her throat.

I was left behind to regret, to grow old in my ignorance.

At any point in those years I might've anonymously returned the stolen *Al Azif* to Miskatonic University. After all, the book was certainly a hoax, most likely written by a fin-de-siècle shyster to profit from the Theosophist craze. It broke my heart to think what stock Scott and Sonia had placed in it. But still I couldn't bear to let it go, and the guilt of being accessory to a crime was a small price to pay.

Then in the spring of 2012, a voice mail message arrived on the phone in my Wilbour Hall office. The speaker was so tentative, I could barely decipher her words, but she gave her name as Patricia Legrasse, widow of retired police detective Raymond Legrasse. I hadn't heard his name since he warned

me away from Sonia Webb in 2001, another life ago. The
phantom noose squeezed tightly again.

When I returned Mrs. Legrasse's call, her tone with me
was almost scornful, like I'd wronged her family in some
way. Ray had died from alcoholism-related liver cirrhosis
two weeks earlier, she told me, and bequeathed to me several
portfolios of written material.

Me? Her voice prickled inside my spine. I felt myself
grasping for a thread of understanding.

Eager to have the papers in hand, I begged her not to put
anything in the mail. "Just get this shit out of my house," she
said, and I was on the front stoop of her Upper West Side
brownstone within five hours.

She answered the door, her features all pulled tight, and
she thrust a heavy leather satchel against my chest. "Keep the
bag. I don't want anything to do with it."

"Mrs. Legrasse, if I've offended you in some way—"

"All you did was hire him."

I opened the satchel on the train back to Providence.
Dread anticipation wouldn't let me dwell on anything else, not
for a minute. Something Sonia told me once came to mind—
about sifting through broken shards to search for meaning.
But she was swept away in a flood with nearly three hundred
thousand others, and this was all I had left for making sense
of my life.

The dossier *was* about Sonia, at least partly: printed
screen shots of her long-defunct *haleysconflict* website, high
school report cards and transcripts from Brown, even a copy
of her birth certificate—April 11th, 1986. Her birth mother's
name was listed, but no father.

Legrasse had followed up on the mother's personal
history. Pregnant at age sixteen, a retail worker in Queens,

now married with two much younger kids—all mundane, all dead-ends.

But wait, had Legrasse ever contacted Sonia directly?

I rifled faster through the pages like all this accumulated detail could somehow soothe my grief. Instead it left me wracked with further questions. My anxious gestures were making the other passengers uneasy. I could feel them watching.

Why had Legrasse gathered so much more than I'd asked of him? He'd traced Sonia's life long after the investigative work was supposed to be done, and he never consulted me again, until now. *In the event of my death....*

He was an investigator, a seeker. I'd put his nose on that website and unchained the collar, set him loose down the path. He was hooked, couldn't stop himself. It was the only explanation that made any sense.

As for why he wanted *me* to inherit his work, I was much less certain. Maybe he wanted to share a discovery, or maybe he wanted me to wallow in the same quicksand I'd kicked him into, all those years ago.

At home I brewed tea and abandoned sleep. Legrasse's investigation had netted my curriculum vitae and tax records, Scott's autopsy report, archival photos of the sculptures and paintings Scott created while at RISD. I hadn't seen these artworks in years—studies of malformation, amphibian and gastropod. They looked impossible yet utterly real.

The photos of Scott's hanged body left me stricken for long minutes. I felt like all my deepest secrets were being stolen from me, and I couldn't fight back. What could I do? These violations were committed years ago by a man now dead.

There were police file copies of Scott's notes, the ones I'd given to Sonia, including the cuneiform dream-script, though the Xerox was hardly legible. Inserted with this "evidence" was a half-literate and inconclusive report from an "Anti-Satanist Task Force" subcontracted by the Providence Police.

The deeper I delved into the files, the more infested with Legrasse's obsessions I became. They swarmed off the page, breeding more and more uncertainties....

In 2003, unable to obtain a local copy of *Al Azif*, Legrasse traveled to the next nearest repository—a university library in Buenos Aires. All that way just to consult a book, a hoax book, the same one that was on my shelf.

After the tsunami, Legrasse booked a flight to Indonesia to trace Sonia's last days. He spent two weeks there. Nothing.

A year later he failed in an attempted border crossing from Jordan to Syria. By then he had been reduced to hounding specious geographical details mentioned in the *Al Azif*, chasing chimeras outside Damascus. I could feel the center losing hold. I stopped calculating the dollars and hours he must've sacrificed.

His widow's resentment struck me afresh.

All you did was hire him.

But what was his holy grail? Some keystone that would hold all these prophecies, fantasies and conspiracies together—some elusive core of truth that could interpret the universe? Whatever it was, he'd died empty-handed.

And yet, tantalizing threads—

A Portuguese poet who'd referenced *Al Azif*, for instance. Several Norwegian-language "fan-zine" articles (translated) involving an Oslo black metal band called Khlûl, whose lyrics were peppered with quotations from the "Mad Arab" Zahr-ad-din, supposed author of *Al Azif*.

For some reason, Legrasse had followed up on neither.

A Google search informed me that the Portuguese poet was five years dead. Khlûl was long disbanded, though recordings of their grating music survived—unrelenting walls of guitar distortion and recording hiss, unintelligibly snarled couplets lifted (via the lyrics sheet) directly from *Al Azif*:

That is not dead which can eternal lie,
And with strange aeons even death may die.

These were minor tremors in my psyche, but one final lead stopped me cold.

In retracing Scott's last months, Legrasse uncovered a brief acquaintance with someone I'd never heard of before: one Philip Wilcox, a New Orleans-based experimental filmmaker who in the mid-1980s used the pretentiously Egyptian-esque stage name *Nyarlathotep*.

Included were publicity photos of Wilcox's Victorian horror shtick: top hat and cane, velvet overcoat. It seemed Wilcox exhibited a few of his short films at RISD in late 1985, and subsequently struck up a friendship with Scott.

By the time Legrasse reached Wilcox by phone in 2005, the filmmaker claimed to have suffered memory loss from drug abuse and a car accident, and insisted he had no recollection of visiting Providence, never mind meeting Scott. Another apparent false lead, except Legrasse's notes expressed skepticism over Wilcox's story—*subject hiding something?*

Before Legrasse could follow up, Katrina struck, and Wilcox dropped out of the picture. It seemed Legrasse didn't even try to track him down, an unusual oversight.

Maybe this was the work he wanted to pass on to me. With a jolt of possibility, I imagined how Sonia might've reacted to the dossier. At times I could almost bend my own thought processes to hers, spotlighting Katrina, and how the hurricane had intervened in this case, almost like it had conscious agency.

Surprisingly, I had no trouble tracing Philip Wilcox to his new Missouri address. He had a blog. There I found contact information, but because Legrasse's phone conversation with Wilcox had been so unproductive, I canceled my Thursday morning class and flew to St. Louis.

Wilcox, retired from his Nyarlathotep persona, insisted we meet at a bar, where he busied himself with a succession of vodka martinis. The man was obese and unkempt. I drank ice water and waited until he was drunk enough before I asked my more pointed questions.

He stuck to his amnesia defense. Having no memory of his three years as an experimental filmmaker, he characterized his films and tour appearances as an elaborate prank enacted by someone else and designed to defame him. If not for the evidence, he'd refuse to believe any of it ever happened.

The films themselves were lost in the flood, or so Wilcox claimed. I pictured rusted film canisters snagged among cypress knees in a bayou somewhere. Before they were swept away, Wilcox had watched the films with a disturbed sense of dislocation, though he was just as baffled by them as anyone else.

"Imagine someone shows up at your door one morning and puts a book in your hands," he said. "You're listed as the author, but you know you didn't write it. It doesn't even *sound* like you. Any idea how that messes with your head? You start thinking there's this secret part of you, deep down, that you can't see. You start wondering who you are, even."

Wilcox described for me the films he had watched repeatedly: long shots of Gulf Coast waters and desert landscapes (he didn't know where) juxtaposed with human shadows acting out gestures both obscene and violent. One film depicted the ritual murder of a young woman by masked figures in a junkyard. Wilcox insisted it showed every sign of having been staged, including, he swore, the dead woman cracking a smile at the end. And no, he didn't know who she was.

In another ten-minute short, young actors, strangers to him, draped their naked bodies with octopus and squid, eventually eating the creatures alive.

"Seems I even had a reel that was just your kid Scott. Up in his art studio up in Providence. It's twenty minutes of him molding some kind of clay figure, like a deep sea creature, kind of. Maybe there's some connection there. It was black and white footage. Like I said, I don't remember shooting it. Hell, I didn't even know who he was till that detective guy Legrasse called me and put two-and-two together. Lost that in the flood, too. Fuckin' shame."

Wilcox had nothing more to offer.

By then, my search had become its own kind of enveloping flood. I was a castaway caught in rising waters that had already taken my son, Sonia Webb, Ray Legrasse. Even Phil Wilcox had succumbed to it, in his own way. I had no reason to believe I'd get any closer to Truth than them. I didn't even know what I was looking for, exactly. But every new step was an exhilarating promise. The quest kept me alive.

Despite my skepticism, I set to work on Scott's cuneiform dream-script from Legrasse's file, first comparing it against all the known Mesopotamian variants, then the wider, less antiquated Middle Eastern scripts, like those of Syria-Palestine from the late second millennium BCE, or the Old Persian Cuneiform, even the undeciphered Proto-Elamite/Linear Elamite scripts.

But if I allowed Scott's script the benefit of the doubt, I'd have to conclude that my comparisons were all too recent, too *evolved* into figurative abstraction or even a fixed alphabet. What he'd drawn was more like the most ancient Sumerian pictographs—tokens, even—the variety of near-literal representations one would expect to find nearly six thousand years ago.

Eventually my pride wore thin enough that I took the dream-script to my colleagues at the annual meeting of the American Oriental Society, in Phoenix that year. They were no help. When I refused to tell them how I'd obtained the script, I was accused of plotting a practical joke. A more acerbic peer said I'd delayed my retirement several years too long.

July 2016 found me at Philadelphia Hilton Garden Inn, preparing to alienate another batch of experts gathered for the Rencontre Assyriologique Internationale. The night before the conference I sat in the lobby with a cup of Earl Gray and perused a stack of magazines left on a side-table.

By that point I'd exhausted, I believed, all the causal relationships Legrasse's file had provided me—so when I happened that evening upon a *Time* magazine article, it was absolute coincidence.

The story was a profile of a controversial Norwegian "prison island" in the Oslo Fjord, where offenders served their sentences in a tranquil natural setting meant to restore their humanity and reduce recidivism. One prisoner, Jørn Enger, was sentenced to the island after having carried out a mass shooting at an Oslo mosque in 2014. I remembered the incident, thirty innocent Syrian immigrants murdered, mostly refugees in search of peace. Just thinking about it sank me into a fog of despair.

But then, the connection. My flagging mind went taut. I felt the rumble in my soul. In an instant, a dozen places and dates across the globe crashed together like tectonic plates, and I was at the epicenter....

Years ago, Enger was the front man for Khlûl, the black metal band described in Legrasse's files.

I tried for more details on my phone, but my fingers trembled too much. Instead I rushed to the hotel business center, where the computer's download speed moved slowly enough to drive me mad. My every muscle ached from roused adrenaline.

Thirty-year-old Jørn Enger was a psychotic murderer and racist, yes, an avowed occultist and white supremacist whose lyrics verified his familiarity with *Al Azif*. But crowning it all was his birth date: April 11th, 1986.

I stared dumbstruck at the monitor display. The motions of the universe were rumbling back around, dragging me helplessly along with their gravitational forces. Fifteen years since I met Sonia, fifteen more since Scott died.

In a translated interview after his arrest, Enger claimed his motive was "to promote the promise of Muslim genocide." But he spouted little of the usual rhetoric about reclaiming Europe for the Aryan race or Christian supremacy. Instead, he wished only to "make Arabia a Paradise again, like forgotten times." His fugues and rants during the trial were largely dismissed as failed attempts at an insanity plea.

Reading about him, I was overcome with regret. I'd read about Enger in Legrasse's file *two years* before he committed mass murder. If only I'd followed the path laid out for me, I might've realized what Enger was. I might've done something— but what?

Even now, what could I do with this revelation? I couldn't just row across the Oslo Fjord, knock on his cabin door, and demand to speak with him. I was seventy years old, easily winded, medicated with blood-thinners to avoid a stroke. I'd let my passport lapse.

So I built a cover story about researching the tenuous links between early Mesopotamian religious belief and neo-Nazi iconography. I wrote to the Norwegian Prosecuting Authority and to reporters at the *Aftenposten*. I wrote Enger's former band-mates, only to learn that one of them had shot himself just after Enger's crime. The other responded via email with a digital photo of male genitalia, presumably his own.

Five times over the course of five months I wrote to Enger himself, with no result. I couldn't sleep from frustration. I couldn't dream the dreams that unveiled the secret world. So I lay in the dark and despaired. Then, one evening after trudging home from campus through a blizzard, I found a letter in my post box, airmailed from Norway.

Inside was a drawing signed in Jørn Enger's hand. It was a mélange of sea creatures, some vaguely octopoid, but others resembled crustaceans and mollusks, long-extinct trilobites. My own hands couldn't hold the paper still.

That night I booked a flight to Oslo. I had no plan in place to contact Enger, no meetings scheduled with the officials surrounding his case. I couldn't even be sure it was Enger who sent me the drawing. But I was driven now by something beyond rational thinking. It was the music of the spheres calling out to my heart. I would commit every resource to this final bid.

Because I *knew* Enger's drawing. I'd lived with it for thirty years. His version was a much more detailed evocation, much purer, but when I mentally abstracted his marine creatures into simpler shapes, darkened the bodies into wedges, what appeared was a prefect replica of Scott's cuneiform dream-sketch.

With days left in the year, I boarded the plane to Norway. It was a cloudless night over the ocean, and north in the Arctic the green wisps of the Aurora Borealis rippled over the curve of the earth like rifts opening wide between the aethers. In a drowse I imagined what might roil up from the deep, just behind that curtain, waiting for its awakening.

There was trouble at customs. The officer brooded over my passport and searched my face before leaving me to stand long minutes at the booth. My back was knotted from hours in the cramped coach seat, and all I wanted was rest. Just as I started to totter, they led me to a blank-walled interview room.

All my Norwegian was from an app I'd studied over the previous two weeks, and none of the *Politi* officers volunteered their English. I was brought coffee and an open-faced sandwich. I was offered bathroom breaks and pitying smiles. But no one would tell me why I was detained.

More than an hour later, a stocky officer tried to rouse me. I cried out, having convinced myself I'd be locked in a holding cell or executed on an unlit airstrip while jets drowned out the noise. "Please, Dr. Angell," she said. "You are called now."

I was loaded into a dark sedan beside another *Politi* with uncannily white-blond hair. He said nothing. We drove through snowfall and towering pine trees, wide fields of darkness. My body still felt thirty thousand feet aloft. I would give myself over to whatever was about to happen....

City lights, then a descent into an underground parking garage. I imagined we were driving into a vast excavation site. But we parked among nondescript cars. Voices echoed, foreign words in puffs of steam. Air so cold I thought my nose would frost over. I was guided by my arm to an elevator. The numbers ticked upward. A man in a Kevlar vest held my suitcase, in which I'd packed the complete Legrasse files.

When the doors opened directly onto a hotel suite, there was soft yellow light and warmth, and I wanted only to melt onto the nearby sofa.

But a woman in this room was saying my name. She wore an imposing dark blazer and pants, but spoke in a reassuring tone, like a nurse. A young black woman with her hair shaved down to a sheen.

"I'm sorry," Sonia told me. "I'm sorry for everything."

III. THE MADNESS ON THE PRISON ISLAND

I TOUCHED HER FACE to be sure it was real. Her eyes glistened but she stood firm with her arms folded behind her back. Thirty years old, and not an outward hint of the incessantly fidgeting kid I remembered. *But Sonia Webb was alive.*

She was also one among a dozen officials present in the suite—Norwegian Intelligence Service, Norwegian Police Security, Interpol, MI6, and a pair of poker-faced Americans who would not give their credentials.

After a few inaudible exchanges in the kitchenette, the others disbursed. Sonia poured us tea and sat in an armchair close by.

"There were reasons...." she began.

She must've assumed I'd be angry, but I'd been through too much to muster any resentment. I felt like a parent whose kidnapped child has been returned to him. Indeed, clarity struck me then and there. She was my daughter. Not biologically, of course, but in a deeper way that we'd been working toward for fifteen years, even when I thought I'd never see her again.

"It's easier to be subtle when you're a ghost...." she said.

She said, "Better for you, George, for your own safety."

Even as I struggled to reconcile this austere woman with the child I knew, I couldn't care about the *reasons*. In a way I couldn't articulate, I'd been searching for her all along, and now I had found her. Or rather she, me.

The sun skirted the horizon from nine to four, a slip of daylight. Room service offered meals, and I slept at intervals. Sonia told me of her own awakening, the morning she was roused from her Sumatran hostel and compelled into the ubiquitous dark sedan. They were *seekers* like her, linked to the international intelligence community. They knew about her website, her amateur investigations. Her trip to Indonesia had finally put her in their immediate orbit.

They'd saved her life, just about plucked her from the swash of the tidal wave. It was, like so much else in her journey, a *coincidence*, a chance to be reborn. At the insistence of this coalition, she cut all contacts, faked her own death—and in return she gained access to their resources, their bureaucratic shortcuts.

As for me, I was a necessary sacrifice, a bumbling old professor without any aptitude. I couldn't cross over the veil.

"That day in Red Hook," I reminisced, "you were convinced I could leverage your membership with the Illuminati, or whatever secret society you thought I represented."

"Go big or go home, right?" she asked.

"Maybe I'll go home. So what are you, then? CIA?"

"Something like that."

When I offered Legrasse's files, Sonia sighed patiently. They'd been familiar with the detective's research at least since he'd crossed one of their associates in Jordan, trying to get into Syria. They'd been forced to block his progress, but they'd also quietly vetted his leads.

I had to wonder how closely I myself had been haunted by spooks since inheriting the dossier, but Sonia would only say that I'd officially "pinged" their alarms with my letter campaign to Norway.

"When you bought your plane ticket, we knew it was time." She stood at the window overlooking the harbor at twilight, where the silhouettes of cargo ships and harbor cranes loomed like Cretaceous beasts. All the distress she once exuded was now locked tightly away.

"It's that bad, is it?"

"The nightmares I've been having. All of us here. Even when I'm awake, I hear the noise stirring through the world. And with the new administration coming, we can't be sure how much longer...it's been getting louder. That's what I'm saying."

"Like New York? Indonesia?"

She gazed out on the waters and said, "This time, they sense it in every corner of the world."

We fell into a contemplative silence. An American associate named Pickman returned with several others for a *debriefing*. Schnapps was poured, though both Sonia and I declined. Glossy photographs of an excavation were passed around. Recent images of an ancient ruin. I could recognize most of the major Middle Eastern archaeological sites, but not this one.

"These were taken two months ago," Sonia explained. "Forty kilometers southeast of Damascus. We think this might've been what Legrasse was looking for—what might be connected to *Al Azif*."

My doubt was a frail thing by then. Whatever I'd believed about that book evaporated in the stark desert light of these findings. The excavation team had exposed an upright cylindrical hollow beneath a supposed burial mound, an inverted tower at least the size of a grain silo, five layers of sunbaked brick plastered around the interior with a brown clay stucco.

There were hundreds of etchings on the clay inner walls. Detail shots revealed what looked at first glance like comets with long outgassing tails. My throat clutched when I realized they depicted marine life. Sonia claimed there were many more etchings than they'd had time to photograph.

"You were there?"

Sonia glanced at Pickman, who nodded some secret approval. She spoke to me in a measured voice, doling out each new fact like a medicine that couldn't be swallowed all at once. If I was being granted secret knowledge, the thrill was swiftly overwhelmed by disquiet.

I didn't deserve this. I had nothing to offer in exchange.

"We were there about a week," Sonia said. "Illegally, and under constant threat of discovery from the Syrian government, Russian spy planes, insurgents—you name it."

On the sixth day, a militia in Toyota SUVs stormed down from the hills and drove the excavation team away with gunfire. Pickman questioned one captured insurgent, who did not identify as a radical jihadist, or any kind of Muslim at all. The man would only insist that the temple was sacred and untouchable.

"Schizo, is what he was," Pickman said. "Bat-shit crazy."

Just then I thought of Wilcox and his amnesia—the lost film footage shot in an unknown desert. He was haunted by the three years he'd wandered in a somnambulist state, at the mercy of some other mind.

"They were *protecting* the site?" I asked.

Pickman shrugged. "There's no logic to it. That tower's been buried for a good nine thousand years, as far as we know. They couldn't have known what they were guarding, not in any rational way."

I looked through the pictures with a mounting certainty that I'd find the unearthed original of the pictographs Enger sent me in the mail. Images that called out from the buried depths of the collective unconscious and cast their echo into the dreamscapes of receptive minds....

Among the skillfully carved totems were cruder gouges, jagged scrape marks in rough vertical patterns down the stucco. Possibly fissures, but they looked more organic, like serpent trails across wet beach sand.

"Nine thousand years?" I asked aloud. They must've known such a date would place this ruin among the oldest signs of civilization in Arabia—or anywhere. The Ubaid Period in Iraq was that old, but nothing this sophisticated remained from that era, certainly not this far from the Fertile Crescent. "Why are you showing me all this?"

Sonia placed one last document on the coffee table in front of me. It was a copy of Jørn Enger's pictographs. "How did you—" I started, but I was being naive. Surely they'd been tracking Enger since the mosque massacre. They could've easily intercepted any mail he sent from the prison island. The more confounding question was why they'd let the drawing carry on to me afterward.

Sonia's people had tried multiple times to communicate with Enger since his arrest. He'd either refused or fallen into a non-communicative fugue state, whether real or feigned they couldn't be sure. After the dig outside Damascus, after Enger produced the drawing, they were all the more desperate to ply the powerful apparatuses of his mind. But he wouldn't cooperate—except with me.

All attending eyes were upon me, except Sonia's. She was gazing out the window again, unwilling to witness my realization. They were banking on the possibility that Enger would talk with me. If not for that, I would've never been invited into this circle. I would never have known she was still alive.

I understood, and still I would do it, whatever Sonia asked.

At dawn the ferry cut through the pale sheets of ice lining the surface of the fjord. I stood on the prow, face to the frigid air. The outdoor chill kept my heart on track.

Sonia came out with the sun, her face wrapped tightly in a scarf, her breath steaming through the fabric folds. The chill was so pervasive it felt crystalline in our lungs. The deck boards were petrified solid.

"What do you think Enger knows?" I asked her.

"He knows what it is—whatever is calling for us."

"What is it saying? Does he know that, too?"

Sonia didn't answer. She watched the ice split apart before the prow, watched the prison island define itself ahead of us, first the sharp peaks of the pine trees, then the rocky shoreline and the brittle winter grass exposed beneath snow drifts.

Ahead at the dock, men lumbered in thick jackets and jumpsuits. Guards and prisoners indistinguishable. Some wore ski goggles and scarves, but the men with faces exposed watched our approach like natives at the first sight of foreigners.

The quaint red cottages peeked through the trees behind them, spouting chimney smoke—and on the hill crest stood a butter yellow meeting house flying the flag of the Scandinavian cross. There was a horse-drawn sleigh sliding up to meet us.

Our group came ashore in a slow procession and stood among the rapists and killers and thieves in the sharp elemental air. There was a taut procedural hesitation. I searched for Enger, but most of the faces were obscured by icy beards.

A discussion ensued. Sonia and I received only a curt English translation. It seemed Enger was in his cabin down shore, awaiting visitors, but the sleigh driver could only carry four of us. Pickman stayed behind, while Sonia and I climbed in with two PST men in black tactical outfits, including holstered guns. Their presence escalated the sense of imminent threat.

The horses drew us along the edge of the island past men hauling wood and ushering cows from the dark of a barn. As I watched, a massive convict drove a splitting maul clean through an upright log. The impact resounded in my chest, and as we passed, the axeman looked on us with blank regard.

I had the unsettled sense that these men had all built this idyllic scene to sedate us, down to the jangling sleigh bells. When I looked to Sonia, she nodded faintly, every muscle on her face alert.

Soon enough the shoreline curve took us out of sight from the dock. We slid to a stop alongside a whitewashed brick chapel. Back here, heavy foot traffic had turned the ground to frozen mud. A man came down a set of crude stone steps, shovel in hand. A black balaclava obscured all but his eyes.

His Norwegian exchange with one of the PST officers sounded increasingly hostile. He made thrusting gestures with the shovel, pointing back up the hill. Sonia smirked at me, a slight hitch in her shoulder. She was trying to put me at ease.

Finally the PST officer explained to us that Enger had only agreed to meet with "the professor," in his cabin. All other visitors would have to stay outside, or wait in the chapel.

Sonia jumped down from the sleigh and addressed the man in the balaclava directly. She moved to within inches of his obscured face, insisting through her teeth that a prisoner of the state should have zero leverage to make demands, that the Norwegian State Police would dictate the terms of this liaison, nobody else.

She was more than a foot shorter than the masked man, and within striking distance of his shovel. I had no idea who he was. He looked down on her with a placid disinterest, like he was watching something dull on television. After half a minute, Sonia shook her head in defeat.

"It's fine," I told her. "It's better I meet with him alone."

"No way. We all go in, or nothing."

"I came all this way. If it's the only way he'll talk—"

She bit her lower lip and glared off toward the hazy mainland we'd left behind. "In case you ever wondered," she muttered. "This is what fucking White Paradise looks like."

"Let me do this," I said, my hand on her shoulder. "We're so close now, Sonia."

She glanced at my intrusive touch and then shook her head in troubled resignation. She said, "Remember everything he says, everything he does. Promise me...."

After that, the whole party took the stone-stepped path toward Enger's cabin. Unremitting stress had already weakened my body, especially my knees. I could barely climb without Sonia's help—my whole being convinced I was headed for the gallows.

The cabin was more of folktale hut, with rosemaled shutters and smoke wisps puffing from the stone chimney. When the door opened, a rush of warm air fogged my glasses at an instant. I ducked inside and saw nothing but steam. The door latched behind me.

I wiped the lenses with the tail of my scarf but even then, the leftover moisture streaked my vision like expressionist art.

Jørn Enger sat before me on the edge of his cot, warming his hands above a pot-bellied stove. The burning wood snapped and hissed. Enger stood upright. The window blinds and my glasses rendered his face an uncertain gray. The room was almost too stifling hot to breathe. I had to anchor my gloved hand against the ceiling to stop from keeling over.

I'd studied pictures of Enger in his black metal days, his matted curtains of hair, his face painted white and daubed with harlequin diamonds. *This* Enger was more subtly unsettling. His undercut was carefully greased, his pressed tan shirt buttoned to the chin. He stood as stiff as a solider at attention. I could not shake the thought of all the death that enveloped him.

The room shrank even further, seemingly, down to the size of a crypt. This was a mistake. I was too old and weak to face this monster, just a blind fool raging against gods. I'd found Sonia and that should've been enough, but I'd let myself believe I was helping her by coming here.

"Why did you send me that pictograph? What does it mean?" I asked him. I was jolted by my own abruptness, like Sonia was somehow speaking through me, demanding answers.

"I knew Scott Angell, your son," he said.

"You couldn't have. He died the day you were born."

"I have seen him in the abyss, where both of us dream." He spoke his English like a practiced recitation, slow and deliberate.

"No more goddamn riddles," I told him.

"You dig through ruins, don't you? You've solved the ciphers of the oldest civilizations. No one has searched as far back as you."

"That's not—"

"*All we ever learn...*" Enger barked. Then he dropped back to a menacing rumble. "...is a single weak spark that gives no light. The godhead thinks no more of our longing than spasms of the billion other beings it has mindlessly spawned."

"Is that why you killed those people? Nihilism?"

"They died for the same reason Scott destroyed himself. Life is not the inverse of death. Life is, after all, only a strange sub-species of dead things."

"What do you know about Scott?" I pleaded, my voice as broken as the rest of my body. My heart flopped against my ribs like a suffocating fish.

"The louse wants to know the nature of the human mind, so he burrows as deep as he can reach, but it's only a scratch on the surface of the scalp. He wants truth. All he gets is a bitter drop of blood."

Woozy from the sauna heat, I had to brace myself against the foot rail on the cot. The truth was asserting its pressure on me ever more in this moment. Enger had confined me here because I was gifted with none of the vision Sonia had. I was easy prey. I was lost before I stepped inside—but still I had to endure, for Sonia. *Remember everything, promise me.*

"You mailed that script. You called for me," I insisted.

"Or they took it from me and sent it, to lure you…to use you for their own purposes."

"What does it mean? Tell me."

"There is no message. Only an echo…."

"What does it want?" I begged.

"It wants nothing. It cries out in the void. It knows no listeners. There is no *it*. There is no call, no invitation. There is only agony. It is only overheard."

I wavered on the edge of consciousness. A chaos of scrape-marks roughed the floor underfoot, cloven hooves. Dark stains in the boards. A spiral staircase in a house in

Providence. There was a time when armies marched to what the haruspex prophesied in sacrificial blood.

Outside the cottage a disturbance arose, an argument, though I couldn't deduce the words. A few gruff shouts and the sonorous thump of horse hooves at a gallop. A frantic whinny.

This whole island was a glamour, some nightmare port in the wanderings of Odysseus. I could sense that we were all under Enger's spell. I had to warn Sonia of the danger, but my voice was caught in my gasping throat, and she felt a hundred miles removed from me....

"I have to...I have to...." I grasped for the door.

As I turned my attention from Enger, another voice in the room with us spoke. "Dad, you have to help me. Dad— please. I can't sleep. Every time I close my eyes, I see it...what does it mean?"

Scott's voice. Even after three decades I recognized it instantly. I pleaded with Enger to stop, but his slit of a mouth kept spilling my child's voice from out of time. "It's symbols. Sumerian, I think, but you would know. You have to interpret it for me, please. It means something. I'm going to go crazy...."

Enger hooked his fingers into his shirt lapels and pulled them apart. The buttons snapped away. His milky, hairless chest was mutilated with raised pink scars in a crude replica of the cuneiform dream-script, as if Enger had used his own flesh as clay.

He wrenched his face into mock desperation. "Please, Daddy, what does it mean?"

A sharp report echoed outside, and then more, and in a paralyzed region of my mind I understood they were gunshots. Fists pounding the outside of the door, Sonia shouting my name.

But the cuneiform scars on Enger's chest had me transfixed, as if the chaos on the island emanated from those wounds, ten thousand years of mindless savagery flooding from underground towers far out in the desert, all of it channeled through Enger and magnified, engulfing us.

He stood over me, barring the doorway. The orange firelight glinted off the blade of a hunting knife that now appeared in his hand. I fell to me knees, and my heart wasn't beating anymore, just quivering its fist-sized store of blood.

"You already know what the Mad Arab tells," he said, stropping the knife against his thigh. "You just won't accept it. All of creation overspills from the dreams of the sleeping godhead, unaware and unconcerned. It's all empty babble, emanating outward. Existence is a nanosecond glitch in the vastness of *nothing*, and you ask me what this means? Every deciphered truth makes man smaller, until there's nothing left. Is that what you want?"

"Don't hurt her. Please don't let them hurt her!"

He pressed the blade against my cheek bone, but I could muster no fear for myself while Sonia was under attack. I imagined those PST men had drawn their guns against her—everyone, all of humankind, in league with Enger.

He paid no mind to the commotion around us, but drew closer and gripped my shoulder to keep me from recoiling, his bare stomach so close I smelled a briny stench like rotting kelp wafting off him. "Look and see the future," he said.

He turned the knife in his palm and drove it to the hilt just below the sternum. His face went slack, jowls shuddering and lips dribbling pink saliva. With a retch I turned away as he sawed the blade down the center of his torso, opening his own flesh like it was simply a coat he could unzip.

The next assault on the door was forceful enough to make the cabin walls tremble. Behind me, a window shattered, and Enger paid no notice. It was all he could do to keep his convulsing body upright. His eyes were empty white, and blood spilled in sheets across his knife hand, and when the pain was finally too much he roared.

The sound was more triumph than pain.

Another blow at the door split the wood planks. An axe head broke through for a moment before it was wrenched away again. They called for me but my mind could make no meaning from the sounds.

Enger let the knife fall to the floor. He spread apart his dripping hands and dropped his chin to marvel at the wound he'd torn in himself. I refused to witness, but his fascination drew me in like the irrevocable pull of an event horizon.

And I saw the answer.

What happened afterward was a strange syncopated flutter of sensations—the cabin door collapsing in a burst of splinters, the sudden rush of cold, a black-clad solider with a plastic face shield, and then Sonia lifting me to my feet as if I were weightless, my limp right arm slung over her back. We rushed out to the gasping snap of cold. Crusted snow crunched underfoot, though my own boots were dragged by their toes as they carried me, Sonia and the *Politi* with a ready gun in his free hand.

Gunshots seemed to crack all over the island as we retreated to the dock. The icy ground drove us ever faster. A prisoner in a red jumpsuit was draped across a tree stump, dazed from unseen injuries, still clutching a claw hammer. He watched us pass like we were apparitions.

"Are you all right?" Sonia asked me, breathless. "What happened in there? What happened?"

Two dead bodies lay face-down in icy pine straw, one of them in dress shoes and slacks—one of ours. On the pebbled shore, a horse lay collapsed with its belly rent open and its wide spew of entrails steaming like smoke from a campfire. Other eviscerated animals lay strewn in their gore, all of them speaking their blood-soaked riddles into the snow, their mad babble.

Just as we came to the dock, a convict lunged toward us, drunk on the uneven pebbles and wrenching at his own beard like some biblical prophet driven wild in the wasteland. I saw the abyss in his eyes and knew that Enger had turned these men with his conjuring. He had made them witness, just as he had done to me.

A rifle blasted and the round bit the rocks just ahead of the crazed man's step. It was a warning shot fired by a crewman on the ferry prow. He pulled back the bolt and readied another shot, but the lunatic had already spun himself inland, chasing shadows that were not us.

Inside the heated passenger cabin, I was draped with a blanket that did little to quell my trembling. Somewhere in the turmoil of getting aboard Sonia had disappeared, and though I wanted to see her safe, Pickman urged me seated on a bench.

A medic tested my blood pressure and fed me pills. He toweled Enger's blood from my face, though the stench of decomposition would not wipe away.

I lashed my head and moaned like an invalid, desperate to escape my own skin, escape my memory of that glimpse inside Jørn Enger. Inside him, where a human anatomy no longer dwelt, but instead something else, something long gestating, something altogether cephalopodan, thrashing and coiling tentacles all sickly white and veined, barbed hooks nestled among suction disks, pale chitinous stalks with madly clasping pincers and serrated strudlitrum that sawed against each other in discordant song, a chaos call ever compounded, ever answered, translucent ribbons and tendrils that seemed to pulse with their own inner light—all of it lashing and seeking toward me, glazing my stupefied face, a madness of fused alien life much more vast than Enger could contain, heaving forth from the confines of his body as if through a portal from somewhere far off, somewhere deep, a place he had found in dreams....

Safe on the retreating ferry, I pressed my cold fingers to my face, where a thin tendril from Enger's birthing had left a welt swollen with some kind of venom, or an infection, or whatever else my weak human flesh couldn't tolerate, not even for an instant. I didn't know what I'd seen. I couldn't decipher what I'd heard. Even now, after such a vision, I was still a sightless fool.

It was oracles like Sonia and Scott who could ever dream of—

"Sonia! Where is Sonia?" I demanded, but she was already there, easing me back onto the bench. She held me in her steady arms and shushed me like I was an infant. All this time I believed I had some expertise or aptitude to offer her, some help, but I was only seeking answers for myself. All I ever wanted was to know.

Sonia held my face in her hands. Her tone was almost cruelly insistent. "George, tell me. Tell me everything." Her eyes were so active and demanding I could see for a moment that fifteen-year-old girl again, the one who rushed toward every clue like the doomsday clock was ticking its last few seconds, and she was the only possible savior.

After all she'd seen, there was still that desperation, just like mine.

"Goddamn it, George—can you hear me?" she pleaded. "Tell me what he said to you. *Please*, you have to tell me what you saw. What you heard. Everything, all of it, *now*...."

Her grip on my head was growing tighter. She didn't understand. I wanted to show her, I wanted her to know, but how? How could I? I had seen the source but there was nothing.

Nothing at all.

DEAR STRANGER

JESSICA ANTHONY

Dear Stranger,

I have your heart. I took it on purpose. It was just lying there on the sidewalk, right at the corner of Washington and Chestnut, all Drained and Puffy-looking. Your heart Looked exactly like a Little beached jellyfish, and seeing it filled me with Sorrow, so I took it. I scooped up your Heart with my bare hands and Put it into an empty Gladware Big Bowl Container leftover from Lunch. Your Heart was barely moving, and I worried that I found it too late, but when the lid snapped, your heart gave me an Earnest pizz ump!

I was filled with JOY. I rushed home as fast as I could.

The first night, your heart slept in my bedroom. I put it between my lamp and alarm cloCk. It wasn't moving at all. I poked it a little. IT didn't Pizzump. "Well, good night," I said to your Heart, and turned off the light.

During the night, I woke up. I heard These strange "Puh-Puh" sounds. Your heart was snoring. It sounded like an old person

Crossing A carpet in Slippers.
The following morning, I sketched your heart at the kitchen table in the Sunlight:

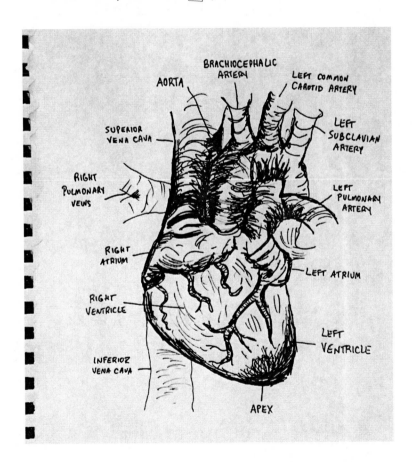

While I was sketching, Your Heart Started slumping. It didn't pizzump and it didn't make any Puh-Puh sounds. "What's wrong with you," I asked, but Your heart said nothing. So I gave youR heart a quick wash in the sink, which seemed to Relax it, and Put your hearT back—nice-n-slippery—into the Glad Ware Big Bowl Container.

I brought Your HEARt To work with me.

I didn't tell anyone about your Heart. But I thought about it eVery second.

I couldn't foCus on anything that Day.

When it was Finally lunchtime, I grabbed my backpack and raced outside. I brought your heart with me to the Royal Botanical Gardens, and we sat on a bench together.

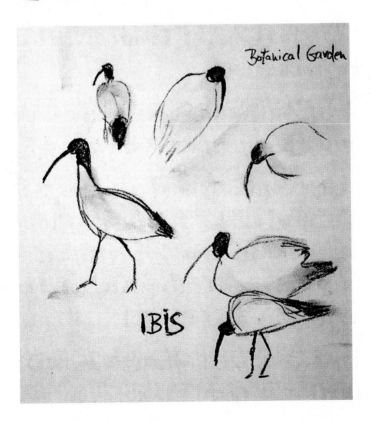

Then, A Funny-Looking biRd walked by.

It was a white bird with a long neCk and A beak like A sCythe. It walked like a Pigeon but it was not a PigeoN.

"What's THAT," I said to No One In Particular.

You Can imagine how Shocked I wAs when your heart answered me.

"That's an IBIS," said your heart. It Coughed a little. "In Turkey, they belieVe the Ibis was tHE FiRst Bird Noah Set free from the ARK. It's a SigN of A Writer's FertiLIty."

I stared at yOUr Heart. "How Do you know ThAt?" I said.

"I belong to A Writer," youR Heart said.

"So you MUST FEEL Things," I said.

"No," said your Heart. "Actually, I Feel VERY little."
Your heart Has not Spoken SINCE.

For nearly a week now, I have kept your heart on the plate in my bedroom. It doesN't want to go into the Big bowl. It doesn't want to Come out. It Does not speak. It occasionally makes pizzump or Puh-Puh sounds.

BuT they Happen less And LESS.

Your heart is aliVe. Your Heart is ALIVE, I ProMise.

But it is dying.

I AM Keeping Your Heart. Just for now. Just Until You get Your shit Together.

I Will Take Good Care of It.

But If you WISH to SeE Your Heart Alive Again, fiX Your Life, you stupid Writer. For the LOVE OF GOD, FIX IT.

Mrs. Hutchinson's Bones

Jason Ockert

THE MORNING OF JUNE 27TH was overcast and gloomy outside the town. Beyond the cobblestone streets the sleepy fields stretched to the bank of the river. Across the water, on the other side, was the forest. Nobody in the village knew what was beyond the trees. Just downstream, at Jackson Falls, water crested over the horizon and dropped two hundred feet to the boulders below. Mist rose from the churning basin.

A flock of grackles skittered out of a cornfield when they sensed the vibrations from thundering footfalls. In platoons they took to the sky, darted across the swift water, and perched in the high branches of sycamore, birch, and pine. From that vantage, as soon as the haze blazed away, they could see everything.

In the village it was clear and sunny. People arrived to the square early for the selection. Though good-natured, a sense of dread clutched at the hearts and throats of the citizens until, finally, everyone learned the name of the chosen one. Then the anxious energy morphed into enthusiastic bloodlust.

This year—which will be the last—Mrs. Hutchinson drew the slip of paper with the coal-black dot. Since she'd participated in many ceremonies she understood what came next. Knowing this didn't stop her from protesting. "It isn't fair," she said as the villagers moved in on her.

That's what they all said—*It isn't fair, it isn't right.* It was the lament of the doomed. Mrs. Hutchinson did what her predecessors always did; she clenched fists, spit, cursed, and punched wildly at her encircling neighbors. The quick children flitted along the periphery and hurled stones with practiced accuracy. From bruised knees the victim ordinarily attempted to talk reason. *If you spare me, I'll mend your fence, Mr. Bentham.* Or, *You can have my chickens, Mr. Graves. I'll paint your barn, Mr. Summers. Mr. Warner, I'll check on you at night from time to time to make sure you're not lonely.* The list was exhausted rather quickly. It was a modest village. There was no bargaining with Nature. As the saying went, "Sacrifice in June, corn grows heavy soon." Mrs. Hutchinson knew this. In fact, she taught it to the children at the schoolhouse. "If you don't follow the path of tradition," she'd lectured, "you stray into ruination. Count your blessings, kids."

Mrs. Hutchinson's blessings were gone. Most sacrifices, after beaten into delirium, hissed prayers through cracked teeth until their final, ragged breath was drawn. The mashed bodies were buried beneath a neat mound of polished quartz (which sparkled in the sunlight) upon a hill upriver which, as everyone in town knew, offered the most spectacular views. From on high you could see thatched rooftops, verdant gardens, and the lucky, bustling inhabitants. Though they rarely visited the burial ground, from time to time townsfolk lifted their heads, massaged their aching lower backs, and squinted up the hill to fondly recollect the men and women who had donated their lives for the betterment of the community.

Unlike the others, Mrs. Hutchinson was not ready to concede defeat. With the deepest conviction she felt—she *knew*—that the process had been tainted. Rigged, even. "It isn't right!" she howled.

Nobody was surprised that Tessie refused to accept her fate with dignity. She was stubborn as a plague of locusts. Always had been. She possessed an unnatural and nuanced rage which made her a fantastic disciplinarian in the classroom but a challenge to interact with around town. If you so much as looked at her the wrong way she was liable to scorch you with a glare and singe you with a sharp word or two. Whether she was born with that fire or taught it as a child was impossible to say. Some folks claimed that she clung too tightly to the notion that they lived in a moral and just world. "Tess," her husband often said, "sometimes things just are what they are."

"You're a damned fool, Bill," Mrs. Hutchinson would reply, even in mixed company. "Good's balanced with evil. Right's squared with wrong. Honor what was and tomorrow'll be better. How could you get up in the morning believing otherwise?"

Most mornings Bill had difficulty getting up, on account of the arthritis.

Tessie's steadfast faith in justice made her volatile in the aftermath of the decision. Her blood boiled with indignation. She just knew, in her bones, that something was wrong. Maybe it was sabotage. Someone could have tampered with that old black box. Surely a dirty worker from the coal company knew the combination to the safe, where Mr. Summers kept it, stole in late last night and tore a tiny corner off the marked slip so that he and his friends could avoid it. Also, Bill had been rushed. "You didn't give him time enough to choose. *Every*body saw that," she said. "If he'd had more time…and why didn't they use wood chips anymore? That's what they used to do. Who changed the rules? Why not return to the old tradition? Life had been better then, if you think about it...and Mr. Delacroix peeked; I saw him, I swear. Where's Clyde Dunbar? His leg was fine. He was limping around the lawn last night. He could have hobbled here and drawn like a man instead of forcing Janey to stand in for him. The slip was meant to be his. I demand a redo!"

Nobody listened to Mrs. Hutchinson. Collectively, they had stopped thinking of her as Mrs. Hutchinson. Her voice, her identity, her history; all of that was stripped away. She was simply the sacrifice. It was better for the children to think this way.

When she was a stone thrower, it was easier for Tessie to believe in fate. As the chosen one, it didn't make sense. If only the mob would give her a few more minutes to think, she'd figure it all out and explain. There was a perfectly reasonable explanation for the mix-up. But time and reason had run out. Her hair unbraided, shoes slipped off, and her jaw nearly came unhinged when she screamed, "It isn't right, it isn't fair!"

Later, Steve Adams, who was on the front line, swore that Tessie's blue eyes flashed scarlet right before she leapt to her feet and shoved the entire crowd a meter back. "She was aided by some powerful evil, that's for sure."

Mrs. Hutchinson broke through the throng, sprinted past the post office and bank, and tore into the fields. Birds scattered. The fleetest teens gave chase. Jack, fast as a fox, took aim, cocked his arm, and threw a stone he'd been sharpening for weeks. That projectile, from fifty feet, shaved a hairy chunk of scalp from the top of Tessie's head. Later, Jack boasted that her noggin looked like it'd been shucked. Held on by the thinnest of ligaments the skin flap wetly flopped against the nape of her neck. After a few dizzy paces the rapid blood loss disoriented the quarry. She stumbled into a tight row of corn and collapsed. Emitting a cry of celebration, the kids decelerated. Several boys trampled a circle in the crop around the victim to make room for the others. It was considered bad luck if you didn't strike the sacrifice with at least one rock and the youth of this village had enough respect for their elders to give them a turn.

Right there, in that precise spot on the earth, was where Tessie would have been bludgeoned to death if it weren't for the grackles. The fog covering the field dissipated and the birds took notice of the violent human affair unfolding in the crops. What did they see? It's impossible to say for sure. Men are not black birds with iridescent wings. What did they do? Well, they didn't swoop low and peck out the eyes of the attackers. They didn't, as a unit, air lift the lightheaded woman to safety. They didn't beckon a pack of snarling wolves. Instead, one grackle simply cawed, *It isn't fair.* Another bird—trees away—replied, *It isn't right.* Soon, the rest of the flock pitched in, calling and responding louder than the rumble of the river. When the message vibrated into Mrs. Hutchinson's blood-crusted ears she muttered, "Yes. True. It isn't." Under a fierce volley of stones she found the courage to stand.

Later, Mrs. Hutchinson's son Davy admitted that he had the strongest urge to tackle his mother and hold her down. Like the other children, he had been taught not to touch the chosen ones or else you might be chosen soon yourself. Even though kids didn't draw until they came of age, they heeded the warning all the same. Since the older children were running out of rocks, Davy handed his pebbles to them and stared at the fleeing sacrifice with his big, blue eyes.

Mrs. Hutchinson careened off of the stalks, staggered out of the field, and waded waist-high into the river. She stood swaying in the water chanting. Nobody but the birds understood what she was saying.

Along the bank were plenty of rocks. Caught up in the thrill of the hunt, Harry pried a slab the size of a newborn hog from the sucking mud. He tottered knee-deep into the water, hoisted the stone above his head, and heaved it at his prey.

Tessie fell face first into the river. The on-lookers let out a cheer that she didn't hear. She didn't swim or kick against the current. Her filthy yellow dress billowed. Blood mixed with water; water with blood. The merciful river carried her over the falls and snuffed out her life on the jagged boulders below. She bobbed in the agitated eddy for a short while before the current tugged her under. Above, the villagers watched her body float away.

"Well," Mr. Summers said. He was nearly out of breath from the chase. "Let's get back to work."

And they did, indeed, return to their lives. They piled a mound of quartz upon the hill next to the other sacrifices. After a while, nobody even remembered that Mrs. Hutchinson wasn't buried there.

The body washed ashore five miles downstream, where the river elbowed. It was a popular place for animals to drink. At dusk, under a sliver of moon, a pair of raccoons discovered the carcass. After a short tussle, the bigger scavenger chased the littler one away. The commotion and tantalizing scent of fresh blood attracted a bobcat. The queen swatted the snarling coon away and dragged her bounty deep into the woods where hungry cubs waited. They feasted on the soft innards all night and left the scraps in a thatch of clover for the vultures.

The carrion-eaters efficiently ripped apart the tough sinew and gristle and gorged. Their stained beaks were painted into smiles. Once they were sated, the rodents scuttled out of holes and crevices. Rat teeth and tongue picked clean all traces of flesh. Then, the insects arrived.

After a few days there was nothing left between Mrs. Hutchinson's skeleton and dust but time. The summer sun baked the earth, autumn gusts stripped the leaves, December snow blanketed the forest floor, and from the wet, vernal earth the fortified clover grew. While people busily buzzed from decision to decision, nothing changed in the woods along the edge of the river a few miles from Jackson Falls.

One summer morning, nearly ten years later, Mrs. Hutchinson's rotting skull released a malevolent force that had been stored in the marrow. Primal hatred Tessie didn't know she possessed was imprinted into her organic bone tissue. It had been dormant in life and in death the fury was waiting to be unleashed by decomposition.

The malice started in the jawbone. Heat crackled from her putrid mandible and set the detritus into which she had settled aflame. The wildfire torched 25,000 acres. It leapt over the river and razed the cornfields and crops which had sustained the village for so long. Ash coated the land in a sulfuric gray blanket. Smoke choked countless animals. Citizens coughed for weeks. Mrs. Hutchinson's bones smoldered.

Once the air cleared, the villagers gathered together and gazed at the open space where the forest used to be. "So that's what's over there," Mr. Summers said from the falls. "It's just like what's over here." He scratched his liver-speckled bald head and said, "Let's get to work."

Many of the early settlers to the new town were miners, carpenters, and factory workers. Horace Dunbar bought three acres of land and moved his wife and son to the new settlement. He planted strawberries and in no time, the ripe fruit leapt from the nutrient-rich soil. Horace should have been happy. He should have appreciated the plentiful yield of the crop. The problem, though, was that he couldn't figure out why one small square of earth remained infertile. The dead patch wasn't particularly large—roughly three-by-three yards—but it happened to fall in the middle of an otherwise robust row. He tried a variety of fertilizers on the soil and tilled it until his fingers bled. Still, nothing. Then one May afternoon when he was over-seeding the spot he had a brain aneurism and collapsed. Through a window in the kitchen back at their house Mrs. Dunbar witnessed her husband clutch his head, drop to his knees, and fall face first into the agitated dirt.

People felt badly for Kitty's loss. Horace was still relatively young and taken—sympathizers cried—before his time. Townsfolk shook their fists at the cruelty of fate. Then, one breezy morning in October the string from a polka-dotted kite was yanked out of eight-year-old Brian Dunbar's clutching hands. From the porch, Mrs. Dunbar watched her son chase the skittering thread over the wilting strawberry plants. Afterwards, Kitty would try to explain what she saw with her own eyes—which people wouldn't believe and in mid-November she'd slit her wrists in the spot where she saw what happened happen—she'd said, "The kite stopped in midair as if waiting for my son." When Brian breathlessly arrived, a microburst whipped up out of the ground and twirled the thread around and around his pale neck until it squeezed the life from the boy.

In the aftermath of the tragedy Betty Zanini, a friend and member of the church to which the Dunbar's belonged, organized a small congregation to hike out into the field and place three wooden crosses where the Dunbar family had perished. A half-dozen people were able to make it. More of the congregation would have attended if it wasn't for a cold snap that had seized the region. After driving the markers into the reluctant ground, everyone prayed. It was so frigid that the words froze the moment they escaped blue lips. In the morning, every one of the mourners woke up without eyesight. Blinded, they couldn't see that the crosses they'd planted had been ripped from the ground and rearranged into bundles of stick figures tied with kite string and littered across the barren field.

These strange phenomena spooked the superstitious citizens and rumor spread that the Dunbar place was cursed. For years, the town grew up around the property. The population expanded and people prospered. The mayor of the modest-sized city decided to use public funds to purchase the old Dunbar farm and convert it into a nice park where families could picnic and throw a football with spirited children. Since the groundskeeper couldn't get any grass to grow over a certain patch of ground, the Planning and Zoning Board simply had a park bench erected over the spot. Upon that bench couples argued, businessmen were mugged, a black widow climbed into a young woman's water bottle, and Mr. Allen choked to death on a hotdog. Soon, the park was abandoned by happy families and inhabited by degenerates. The police chief, whose grandfather was a founding father of the city, lost count of the number of alcoholics and drug addicts who expired in a gurgle of despair upon that bench.

In an effort to turn the negative space into a positive one, Mayor Graves paved a large portion of the park and built a library. Other than one incident—a construction worker was crushed by a pile of lumber that had been poorly stacked—the Jackson Public Library was completed on schedule. It opened on a sunny morning in late June.

Inside, the smell of fresh paint and new books permeated the bright air. Children paged through vividly-colored picture books while adults browsed the best sellers. A modest crowd milled through the stacks and fingered the spines of hardbacks.

Toward the rear of the library, in the media room, were several computers. Each monitor rested in its own partitioned carousel to provide privacy. This section soon became the most popular area of the library. Although everyone had their own computer at home, there was something that drew them to the media room. People could browse however they chose without having their IP address traced. There was freedom in the anonymity. The space became so popular that patrons would camp in front of the monitors all day. Under a volley of complaints, Ms. Percy, the librarian, had to set a two hour time limit so that everyone could have a turn.

Over one particular computer station the florescent light always flickered. The maintenance workers couldn't figure out why. They replaced the bulb and rerouted the wires and still the light blinked and hissed. "It's the darndest thing," said Mr. Overdyke, scratching his bulbous nose. "There's nothing at all wrong with it. Just don't want to work right."

People didn't mind. In fact, many visitors preferred to sit at that particular station. Half-lit, the area afforded additional privacy. Plus, the low, erratic, eruption of sound was oddly pleasant. It was familiar and peaceful like distant traffic. Users incubated in a comfortable numb.

If someone had the willpower to shift their attention from the screen and actually listen, they might detect a pattern bleating from the flashing light and buzzing static. If they allowed the vibrations to trickle into their ears, they might detect a broadcast; an electronic cry on an endless loop: *It isn't fair. It isn't right.*

Nobody heard the message. Nobody mustered the courage to stand, power down the computer, flip the light switch off and sprint outside into the vast open world.

Instead, citizens parked in front of that one particular computer and trolled the internet. Mrs. Martin, a spritely octogenarian who'd outlasted four husbands, teetered to the computer each morning at 8:45. She set her ebony cane against the wall beside her and visited www.sewimpressive. com. The site was created for the modern seamstress. On it, you could learn new patterns, best stitching practices, and tips for accurate sewing. Because building a community was important to the woman who hosted the site, there was a blog where people shared stories and pictures. That's where Mrs. Martin spent her time. Hunting and pecking for the right keys on the keyboard, she would reply to a picture that a seamstress had proudly posted by writing: *Mrs.SewandSew, the thumbs in your mittens are lop-sided. Maybe you should try a different hobby, dear.* To this insult, Mrs.SewandSew responded: *I'm trying my best, BadBird5000. And for your information, my husband loves my sewing. He's wearing the mittens right now and says he can't wait for it to get cold!* Mrs. Martin, shielded by her alias, wrote: *You must have stitched your husband's eyelids shut because he'd have to be blind to think you had any talent. He's also having an affair with your sister and feels sorry for you.* Mrs. SewandSew replied: *You are rude and inappropriate. Shame on you! You don't know anything about me. I'm reporting you to the webmaster.* Excitedly, Mrs. Martin wrote as quickly as her old fingers could clack: *Die! Die! Die! You stupid bitch!* And then the community portion of the site shut down and Mrs. Martin would visit another site like www.stitchsewgood.com and scroll down the comments section.

Eventually, the librarian would gently tap Mrs. Martin on the shoulder and inform her that her time was up. A line was forming. "Oh," she'd say, pulled from her trance. "Time passes so fast."

The moment Mrs. Martin was gone the next visitor slid into the still-warm seat. It could be Mr. Anderson, who hated felines, up next. He'd search pictures of cats or kittens on social media. The happy pet owner might post a photograph of a tortoiseshell-coated tom chasing its tail with a note that read: *Keep trying, Fritzy, you can do it!* To this, Mr. Anderson would copy and paste an image of a bagful of cat carcasses along a muddy riverbank attached with the note: *I'm coming for your pussy.* When his time expired, Joey Watson would take his place. Except for the two hours allotted to him while he sat at the public computer, Joey really wasn't a racist. Barbara Jones was *IHateU351.* She blasted romance novels she'd never read on GoodReading.com and enjoyed calling both authors and readers fat sluts. Greg Clark, who showed up in the late afternoon, took great pains to replace lyrics and graphics to popular children's tunes. He'd re-record songs and post them on YourTube. If a kid decided to click on "Row, Row, Row Your Boat," they might be exposed to: "Row, row, row your butt, gently with a spoon. Merrily, merrily, merrily, merrily, anal sex is fun!" while pornographic images interrupted the otherwise pleasant video. Parents complained like hell in the comments section.

Old Man Warner was usually the last in line. He stood fidgeting just outside the circle of humming light. When it was finally his turn he'd scour the web for obituaries and write, where grievers expressed sympathies for the families and friends of the deceased: *I'm thankful that your loved one is gone. It's your fault. You should be ashamed. The dead will hate you for all eternity.* Beneath his feet, beyond the carpet, concrete, and dirt, Mrs. Hutchinson's bones radiated as they slowly decomposed. There was no hope for him until they turned to dust.

Though Old Man Warner and the rest of the users would never know it, the vicious remarks they made spread seeds of malice across the planet. The victims might be angry, at first, and cry, "What kind of person could ever write something so mean?" Certainly not them. After a while, once they calmed down, they would grow despondent. They'd quit visiting the sites that once gave them pleasure. They might ride a bike, go fishing, or work on a crossword puzzle; anything to keep their minds preoccupied. Sooner or later, though, their resolve would begin to crack. They'd start to resent the faceless monsters that spoiled their enjoyment. "How dare they take away my freedom," they might say to themselves. Then, one by one, they'd get their revenge by visiting the local library and waiting in line for their turn at the public computer. They'd chisel words into stones and hurl them into cyberspace. When they hit their mark—when a person responded with indignation—they'd emit a restrained squeal of delight and redouble their efforts. Afterwards, they wouldn't feel good, but they'd feel justified.

Around nine pm, the Jackson Public Library closed. The janitor rearranged chairs, emptied trash cans, swept the floors, extinguished the lights, and locked the front door. Back home, everyone did what they always did: watched television, ate a bowl of ice cream, brushed teeth, and went to bed. In dreams, their guilty ancestors maddeningly chattered. In the morning, a crowd gathered on the marble steps of the library. Citizens exchanged pleasantries and kept a close watch on the entrance. When the door was thrown wide, there was a wild rush past the towering stacks of dusty classics, around the children's craft table, and into the media room. Pushing and shoving, the meekest screamed, "No fair, I was here first!"

Nobody ever listened. Once the mob spotted the computer beneath the epileptic overhead light they were upon it.

The Other Neighbors

Brian Evenson

So, we had to go out of town. Not me so much, but Jim—
he works for a machine parts place and when they call and say
Jim, head on over to Cheyenne and see about such and such, well,
he does. And that was what they said.

So, we were lying in bed and Jim said, "Honey, do you want
to come?"

And I said, "Cheyenne, you mean? Jim, you've got to be
shitting me. Why would I want to go to Cheyenne?"

But then he began to sweeten the pot. Not just Cheyenne,
he said, kissing me on my bare shoulder—sure he had to go to
Cheyenne but that'd be just a day, two tops. After that, since we
were already out there and St. Louis was basically just around
the corner so to speak we could go to see Janey and Karl.

"It's like a twelve hour drive from Cheyenne to St. Louis," I
said. "That's hardly right around the corner."

"Who said anything about driving?" he said. "We'll fly, go
in style, babe."

"Keep talking," I said.

By the time we were done, it was a couple days in
Cheyenne and a week's vacation in St. Louis, and I was most
definitely in.

"But what about the cat?" I asked. "We've got to get someone to watch Kitty."

His brow creased and almost immediately smoothed out. He goes, "Sure. We get the neighbors to do it."

"Which neighbors?" I asked.

"You know," he said, "the new folks across the hall. The ones in 2B. The whatchamacallits, you know, the...Millers. Get them to drop in and watch the cat."

"Honey, we hardly know them," I said.

"It's housesitting, not rocket science. Not even housesitting when it comes down to that—just apartment watching. What could go wrong?"

So the next evening before Jim got home I went over and knocked on their door, three cans of Pabst dangling from an otherwise empty six-pack yoke, and they invited me in. Bill, his name was, and hers was Arlene. The Millers. He was a bookkeeper, worked for a firm downtown. She did some sort of secretarial thing—she started to explain then stopped, deciding, I guess that it wasn't interesting.

When I told them what we wanted, what we were hoping for, they kind of looked at one another, blinking. "What do you think, Arlene?" Bill said half under his breath, and then, before she had a chance to answer, said, "Sure, of course we'll do it. Happy to help." He was an odd one, and I should have realized it right there. Instead, I gave him the key, gave them instructions for feeding Kitty, told them how often to water the plants, let them know our schedule, and left.

The trip itself went just fine. Jim, whatever else he is, isn't a liar, and he managed to get us the hell out of Cheyenne on schedule.

Then it was seven days in St. Louis, which was hot and muggy but no worse than home, and, like us, Janey and Karl had air conditioning, which meant that whenever it got to be more than we could take we just went inside and turned it up.

It was a good trip all in all. A lot of drinking admittedly, but that's how it always is with Janey and Karl. Some playing around too, with Jim drunk enough the first night to get sloppy with Janey in the kitchen, but Karl just took that correctly as a sign to cozy up to me and then everybody was happy. Before you knew it, well, let's just say that we woke up hung over and all in the same bed. It was awkward at first, but pretty quick Jim was making johnny cakes and cracking wise and we were all laughing it off and blaming the liquor and everything was okay, no harm done. Just like it always is with Janey and Karl. The nights after that just got better and better, which made it so that at the end we almost didn't want to go home.

But we did go home. And who were we kidding? Jim and I always had a great time just the two of us, and it was only better after a little fooling around with Janey and Karl. On the last night, we'd gotten them to agree to pictures again, as long as we promised to send them copies, so we were going home with a few rolls of shots to develop and add to the collection. It'd give us something to look at, something to reminisce about, something to get us going.

And there we were, home: off the plane, back by taxi to the building, trudging up with our bags, two o'clock in the afternoon. We got to the door and Jim got out his key—I'd given mine to the Millers, we didn't have a spare—and put it in the lock. But the key wouldn't turn, the lock wouldn't open and when Jim bent down and took a closer look he said, *This isn't our lock.*

"What do you mean it's not our lock?" I said. "It's our door, isn't it?"

Jim peered at the number on the door and then peered around the hall like he was in a bad dream and then finally said, "Yes, I guess it is. But somebody's changed the goddam lock."

I tried it too and damned if he wasn't right. But who would have changed the lock?

"You paid the rent, right?" I asked.

"Sure," said Jim. "We were just gone for ten days. He'd at least give us a warning even if I hadn't."

"Must be the Millers, then. God knows what happened. Not rocket science, eh?" I said. "Well..." and I walked over and pounded on the Millers' door.

But it was the middle of the day. Nobody answered. They were at work, I told myself.

"What do we do now?" I asked Jim.

He shrugged. "Wait until they get home," he said. So we sat down in the hall, our backs against the wall, and waited.

We were expecting to hear the sound of the front door opening downstairs, then their voices maybe, then the sound of their footsteps coming up the stairs. Which made it all the more surprising, when all we heard was a door opening in our hall. Their door, we thought at first. But it wasn't their door opening: it was ours.

There they were, Bill and Arlene, just for a brief glance before they realized we were there in the hall and slammed the door.

"What the fuck?" said Jim, scrambling to his feet.

"Was he wearing your shirt?" I asked. "The Hawaiian one?"

"Hell yes," he said. "And my shorts too. Or their twins."

"She was wearing my blouse," I said. "I'm sure it was my blouse."

"How sure?" asked Jim.

"A hundred percent," I said.

His jaw tightened. He started knocking on the door, but they didn't answer.

"Bill?" he said. "Arlene? Come on out, guys!"

He kept knocking, then waiting for an answer and then knocking again. What the hell? Did they think they could just wait us out? That eventually we'd go away?

When they finally came to the door, they were dressed differently, in their normal clothes. He looked like an accountant and she looked like a secretary again, rather than like people who had just come back from vacation. "So sorry," Bill said. "We were just in the middle of feeding the cat."

"Is that so," said Jim flatly. "What were you doing in my clothes?"

"What do you mean?" said Bill. "What are you talking about?"

Jim started to speak again, loud and hoarse, and I could see the way the muscle in his jaw was working that things were going to get quickly out of hand. I reached out and touched his arm, and stopped him.

"Honey," I said, "we don't need to worry about this. We're just glad to be home." I turned to Bill and Arlene. "Thank you for watching the cat."

Bill nodded. "Happy to do it. Call on us anytime."

"Not fucking likely," said Jim.

"We're tired," I said. "Long flight. We're not at our best. You'll have to excuse us."

It was Arlene who took the hint. "These people need to rest, Bill," she said. "We should leave them to it. Give them the key."

Bill reached a hand into his pocket and froze. "I," he said. "I don't know where..." he trailed off, and glanced behind him into the apartment. "I just left it inside, let me go back in and grab—"

But Jim already had an arm around Bill's shoulders and was steering him out. "No need," he said. "We'll find it." He brought his face close to Bill's, stared right into his eyes. "How about you explain what happened to the lock?"

"We accidentally locked the key in," said Arlene quickly. "Bill did, anyway. We had to break the lock open and then call someone to replace it with a new one. We had to pretend to be you, otherwise they never would have done it," and then for some reason she giggled.

Jim was fuming as he shut the door and turned the deadbolt. "They're lying to us," he said.

"Of course they are," I said.

"They probably kept a key for themselves," he said. "And where's ours anyway?" We looked on the table, the counters, but the key was nowhere to be seen. The plants were not dead but not thriving either. Kitty was in the bathroom, the door closed. His food bowl was in there too, and I could tell by the hair gathered on the rim of the toilet that he'd been drinking from it. From how eager he was to get out, it seemed like he'd been shut in there a long time, days maybe.

Jim was still looking for the key, going through the cupboards now. I just went into the closet. All the clothing it, all in disarray. I

g and reached into

.. .act, one for each of us.

... our liquor too," Jim said, shaking a nearly
...pty bottle of Chivas Regal in my general direction.

What a disaster. By the time we'd gone through the place we realized that they'd rearranged everything in the cabinets. They'd left a pitcher in the middle of the living room floor, god knows why. And a bottle of my pills were gone—nothing I needed, and expired, but still. The bed was poorly made, obviously slept in. Plus, there was a brown and shriveled apple core under the nightstand, and someone had taken two bites out of the cheddar in the fridge. I mean who the hell does that? You could see the teeth marks right on it.

Plus, they'd found our pictures, the ones we'd taken with Janey and Karl, and with some of our other couple friends too. They'd pawed all through them, mixed them up, got their fingerprints all over them. I mean, sure, people are curious, anybody would look through a stranger's house given the chance, but most people are smart enough not to be so obvious about it.

First thing we did was have the lock rekeyed, just in case they'd kept a key. After that, we washed or dry-cleaned all the clothes, washed the sheets, put things back in as much order as we could. For a good month, we ignored the Millers, didn't speak to them at all, made a point not to go out into the hall if they were there, made a point to turn around and go back outside if we were coming into the building and heard them coming down the stairs.

But you can't do that forever. I mean, it felt like we were living as prisoners in our own apartment. It didn't bother

Jim as much since he was gone at work all day, but it started getting to me. Either we had to find a way to get over it or we had to move.

And so eventually I said hi to Arlene when I was down getting my mail. Nothing big, just one word, and when she wanted to have a conversation after I just said I had to go, but that was a start. Pretty soon, we were nodding at one another in the hall, and Bill was nodding too. Jim at first wasn't on board, but finally he just rolled his eyes and said, "At least they didn't kill the fucking cat," and was civil to them.

Another month and we'd pretty much gotten over it. Sure, we weren't going to have them housesit for us, weren't interested in doing anything with them, but we could have a quick conversation with them in the hall and act like everything was normal. Which, in a way, made everything seem like it *was* normal.

Which was why, when I saw Bill through the Judas knocking one afternoon when Jim was out, I opened the door.

"What can I do for you Bill?" I asked.

"Harriet," he said, "It's like this." And then he told me.

"So you mean to tell me," said Jim late that night in bed, "that he wanted to offer us money?"

I nodded.

"How much?" he said.

I swatted him. "You're not going to take it," I said.

"Of course not," he said, hands up in surrender. "What do you take me for?" And then, he grinned. "How much was it again?"

So I told him. He whistled. "You've got to have it wrong," he said. "That'd cover a year of our rent."

"No, that's the number. It's his savings," I said. "All of it, I think. Or most of it anyway."

Jim wrinkled his brow. "Are you sure they don't just want to swing with us?" he said. "Play around a little? And want to pay for it for some reason? I mean, they're not my type, but that at least would make sense."

I shook my head. "Bill was very clear," I said. And when he didn't believe me, I told it to him again: Bill had proposed swapping apartments. Not forever, just for a month. We would leave all of our things just as they were. For a month we would live their life and they would live ours. Bill was about the same size as Jim and I was the same size, more or less, as Arlene, so we would just wear one another's clothes. We'd still go to our normal jobs and all that, but back at the apartment we would be them and they would be us. We'd even swap names. And then, after a month, we would go back to living our own lives. "Why?" I had asked Bill. "What would be the point?" Bill had just shrugged. "Just for fun," was the best he could come up with.

"What are they really up to?" Jim wondered. He said it in a way that made it clear he wasn't really asking me, so I just left him to wonder.

Which in the end was a mistake, since it got his curiosity up.

Which was why he eventually said yes and convinced me to say yes too, and so started in motion events that would lead to Bill's confinement in a closed ward and Arlene moving in with Jim and insisting that he call her by my name.

Me, I'm on my own and happier that way. Or so I tell myself. But that's another story.

Tricoter

Joe Oestreich

WE'D LOOKED AT THINGS. We'd tried new drinks. But this morning Kate and I didn't feel up to mingling with the clear-eyed, spring-stepping window shoppers of the Rue des Abbesses. We had no interest in seeing our hangovers reflected back at us in the pink faces of the Montmartre's boulangerie and pâtisserie patrons, they of the ever-fashionable Burberry plaid. So we lowered our eyes to the sidewalk and followed the pressure in our frontal lobes to the dimly lit, wood paneled Café Le Baroudeur—the kind of place where you can order a beer before noon and not feel guilty. Kate and I are perched on stools at the first table by the window. On the other side of the glass, the Place des Abbesses is dolled-up with décorations de Noël. It's eight days until Christmas, and a blue sky hangs over Paris for the first time since we arrived here a week ago. But the Café Le Baroudeur is smoky as a bowling alley on league night. Above our table a sliver of sunlight plays tricks with the floating ash. Kate is rummaging through her bag, looking for her knitting needles. I'm writing in my journal. We're not speaking presently. Well, Kate's not anyway.

"You want coffee?" I say, running my tongue across the sweaters of my teeth.

Kate's attention is focused on the scarf she's knitting my dad for Christmas. "Whatever," she says.

I motion toward the bartender, "Deux cafés-au-lait, s'il vous plait."

He brings the coffees on a serving tray. Two cups, two saucers, and a few Euro-long sugar packets with "Lavazza" printed on the side. I turn one of these packets end over end. The granules flow down and then down again: from L to A and A to L and back. Kate's hands are a tangle of silver needles and alpaca wool. I watch her fingers go through their calisthenics. Pull yarn-Wrap around-Push through-Yank off. Purl stitch. Knit stitch. Purl stitch.

"What's wrong?" I say, tearing open the sugar and pouring it over my coffee.

Kate doesn't look up from her knitting. "Nothing." *Pull yarn.*

"Do you want to—"

"I don't want to talk. I'm fine." *Wrap around.*

"Look. I'm sorry I dragged you across half of Paris last night. I had no idea the Metro quit running—"

"It's not that." *Push through. Yank off.*

I drop my palms to the table, and my wedding ring makes a popping sound on the dark wood. "What is it then?"

"Nothing." *Purl stitch. Knit stitch. Purl stitch.*

Open on the table before me is an unlined Moleskine—the notebook allegedly used by the turn of the century Parisian avant-garde. I know it's ridiculous to think I can channel the intellectual magic of the Lost Generation simply by heading to Barnes and Noble and buying the journal with proper literary bloodlines. And yet, here I am: an Ohioan in Paris who likes to think of himself as the type Hemingway, Gertrude Stein, and Sherwood Anderson would have saved a seat for at Les Deux Magots.

I'm eighty-five years late for my swig at the Absinthe bottle. The crumbs of that movable feast have long been swept up. But across the Seine, the Place St. Germain des Prés—a boutique-lined intersection that patrons of Les Deux Magots gaze upon from behind their 6.00 € chocolat chauds—continues to cash-in on its artistic and intellectual past. Tourists from around the world descend on that hollowed spot in La Rive Gauche hoping to get a nose full of the air expelled by Sartre, de Beauvoir, and Picasso, luminaries whom if they were alive today would surely take one sideways glance at Les Deux Magots' distinctly un-bohemian clientele and decide to just walk on by. Hemingway would never stand shoulder to shoulder at the bar with the tour-bus set, forced to share an ashtray with Mitch and Helen Baughman of the Bloomfield Hills Baughmans—Mitch, a mid-level purchasing executive at Ford, and Helen, a retired middle school teacher with snowmen and candy canes appliquéd to her sweater. It's the same at all the old haunts. Le Café de Flore? The Baughmans have been there. Harry's Bar? The Baughmans have done that. The American Bar at La Closerie des Lilas? The Baughmans have already FedEx'd the souvenir t-shirt home to their son Trevor, a sophomore at Michigan State. *Once they take it away, Papa,* I think, hunched over my journal, *you never get it back.*

At the Café Le Baroudeur's mahogany bar, an old-timer *clink-clanks* a demitasse cup against its saucer to signal that he's ready for another espresso. Except for a pencil-thin moustache, his face is two or three days unshaven and lined with stubble the color of gourmet pepper: a patchy dash of reds, blacks, and grays. Is he a rough forty or a well-preserved sixty? He's wearing a long-out-of-fashion double-breasted suit and dirty Nikes, but he has accessorized this outfit with such strange, dandified flourishes that he maintains an air of superiority, like he's the last-standing sophisticate in the 18th Arrondissement. His dapper felt hat is cocked just-so, the brim turned down in front and up in back to reveal the scruff of an untrimmed neck. The tailored but wrinkled flannel suit hanging on his wiry frame speaks of an impoverished elegance, of a history of fuck-ups so glorious as not to be believed by mere civilians.

This Bum-Dandy of the Rue des Abbesses is standing at the bar, but he's not leaning on it. He won't stay still long enough to put his weight on any singular point. His movements are multi-hinged, like a puppet's or a break-dancer's—herky-jerky rather than fluid, a series of snaps and pops and petit mal seizures. And yet this is somehow graceful, not in the calculated manner of a drunk feigning sobriety, but more like a colt shaking off the sleep of the womb. His limbs seem to unfold in all directions at once. For the Bum-Dandy, a routine gesture like digging in his pocket for change is a dance that starts at his running shoes and shivers up his caffeinated legs, through his torso, and over and around the balls and sockets of the four extra joints he seems to have in each arm. As his left hand descends into his trouser pocket, his legs shuck and jive, and his right hand buzzes from belt buckle, to lapel, to hat brim, to left elbow, and back to lapel before resting on his hip long enough to counterbalance the weight of the change being extracted from the opposite pocket. The coins hit the counter just as the bartender swoops in to deliver espresso shot number two.

"Bite…pain…choke…a lot?"

I reel my stare back to across-the-table distance. Unlike the other women in the café, Kate's not wearing makeup. Her skin is winter break-pale, made even more so by her short black hair. With the sun on her freckles, she looks younger than she did five and a half years ago on the day we were married. "What was that?" I ask.

"I said, 'Do you want a bite of *pain au chocolat?*'" She goes back to her needles and wool.

"You can have it," I say.

"I'm not hungry." *Pull yarn.*

"Look. I can tell you're not fine, so do you want to talk about it or—"

"Not really." *Wrap around.*

"But what—"

"It's nothing, Joe." *Push through.*

"Then why—"

"See, if you don't know, then that's part of the problem." *Yank off.*

"Don't know what? What are you talking about?"

Kate's needles stop cold. "Did you mean what you said last night?"

Last night: French graffiti etched into wooden tables, the words worn smooth by palm sweat and spillover beer. Puke and piss in a urinal stall that wouldn't stop rolling back and forth. Garbage-strewn streets on the long walk back to our 30.00 € hotel.

I take a slurp of coffee and drop the cup down on the saucer, maybe a little too heavily. "What did I say?"

"Never mind," she says.

"How can I know if I meant it, if I don't remember what I said?"

"Now isn't a good time."

"Huh?"

"'Now isn't a good time.' That's what you said."

"A good time for what?"
Kate looks me right in the eyes. "C'mon, Joe," she says.
"What? Do you have something to tell me?"
"Would it matter if I did?"

The Bum-Dandy lights a Gitane cigarette and turns away from
the bar to face the tables. He's sporting a maroon tie, but it's
not around his neck. His conventionally worn tie, his *necktie*,
is blue with gold fleurs-de-lis, but this maroon one is tucked
into his breast pocket, doing the jaunty work of a kerchief.
He's also wearing two belts. The first is dressy and black,
and it snakes around his waistline. The other is down below
his hips. It's brown with a big, Country-Western buckle of
rhinestones and turquoise. Dangling from his right hand is a
small, twine-handled shopping bag that in some past life might
have carried a jewelry box—a buttery case that promised to
snap open to pledges of love and honor and such. Today the
crumpled bag is grimy from his cigarette-ashed hands, and it
looks like it might contain a scraggily toothbrush or a pair of
soiled underpants. But the Bum-Dandy reaches into the bag
and takes out a fistful of bright-white tissue paper tied loosely
with a red ribbon. He holds the package gently. At the edges.
The half-smoked cigarette rests in the corner of his mouth as he
pulls the ribbon tight. A wisp of smoke seeps through his lips
and is immediately drawn in by his nostrils. Having secured
the package to his satisfaction, he looks around the bar, slowly,
as if taking an inventory. His eyes meet mine, and he drops the
package into the bag. He shoots me an espresso-stained smile.
I'm worried that he has caught me sizing him up.

"So *are* you, Kate?" I take a bite of the chocolate croissant
after all—a calculated attempt to appear nonchalant.

"I'm not." She turns her wedding ring in slow circles around her finger. "But what would you say?"

"If you were?"

"Yeah."

"I'd say, 'Oh my god. Great. Fantastic. Let's celebrate.'"

"Last night you said, 'Now's not a good time.'"

I rub my eyes with the heels of my hands and think about our lives back home in Columbus: the two of us in grad school, both with student loans, living in our cramped apartment. "But you *weren't* last night, Kate."

"I'm not now."

"Right. Good." I lick a flake of pastry from the corner of my mouth.

"There's never a good *time*, you know. There's only the time you either decide to or decide not to."

"Then why now?" I say. I'm stirring the dregs of my coffee with the miniature spoon. "Why all these hypothetical—"

"It's not hypothetical."

"But you're *not*."

She jabs her knitting needles into the air for emphasis. "That's not the point."

"What's the point, then?"

"The point is you don't know *what* you want. You think you do, but—"

"What do you mean? I've said all along—"

"Now I don't even know if—" Kate sets the needles down on the table and runs her fingers over her forehead and temples. "I'm just tired, Joe. I'm just really tired."

"You're always tired."

The Bum-Dandy drags his Gitane down to the filter, drops the butt into his espresso shot, and gathers himself as if to leave. He pats down his pockets, and nodding *adieu* to nobody in particular, he points himself toward the front door. His legs fold and un-fold. He dances his Bum-Dandy dance. But before he reaches the exit, he shudders to a stop—right beside Kate and me. All his greasy pistons and gears grind down to zero, and he just stands there with his bag in his hand, looking into the space between us.

He clears his throat and gestures through the window. "Regardez là-bas," he says. *Look over there.* His voice is like wet coffee grounds.

We turn and look. Christmastime in the Place des Abbesses. Bells ring in the tower of Saint-Jean l'Evangéliste church. Fur-coated women with big, black sunglasses and architectural heels manipulate the stairs of the Metro stop. A gaggle of tourists marches up the hill toward the Sacré Coeur.

Then I see what he must be pointing toward: a carousel, golden in the sun. Five or six kids with puffy jackets scatter from horse to horse trying to land a prize stallion. The littlest ones are boosted up onto their mounts by parents who give last-minute words of encouragement.

And they're off.

The ride lurches forward. Tiny mittens clutch plastic-molded reins. Scarves become riding crops, lashing at sinew and bone in an effort to eek out just a little more speed. Shoulder-length hair whips in the wind as horses and jockeys disappear 'round the backstretch. The parents hover in small groups with their hands in their pockets. They smoke and gossip and plan the business of the day. They shake their heads and mutter at the headlines. They check their watches, worried that they've missed their trains. And the carousel spins and spins. This is a race won by everyone and no one.

The Bum-Dandy lets out a long breath. "C'est magnifique," he says, and he looks down into Kate's lap. "Que faites-vous?" *What are you making?*

Kate wraps the half-scarf around her neck and rubs her arms in a fake shiver.

"Ahhhh...un écharpe," says the Bum-Dandy. A scarf. He purses his lips to let Kate know he's impressed. "C'est très bonne." It's very nice.

"Un écharpe?" she says, trying the word on for size.

"Oui. Parfait."

Kate raises the needles and the skein of wool. "Knitting," she says, miming a few stitches. "Comment dit-on en Français?" *How do you say this in French?*

"Crochet," he says, bending his index finger into the shape of a crochet hook. Then he shakes his head and frowns. "Non...non." His eyes widen. "Tricoter! Oui, je pense qu'il est le mot. Tricoter."

"Tricoter."

"Exactement, madame." He smiles from Kate to me and back again. "Tricoter."

I reach over and rub the back of Kate's hand with my thumb. I turn toward the Bum-Dandy and nod to say, *I understand. Thank you.*

And then he steps away. But he doesn't leave the cafe. He heads back to his spot at the bar, back to his demitasse cup and saucer. "Tricoter!" he says, loud enough to be heard over the laughter and the arguments and the clinking of forks and knives and Stella Artois glasses. Looking down into his cup, he snorts at the cigarette filter soaking up the last sip of espresso, and he tucks his shopping bag into his suit pocket.

I hope whatever is in that package is clean and new. A porcelain ballerina. A miniature Formula 1 car. A gift for someone who will come running when this man shows up at the door.

To Build a Fire

Stefan Kiesbye

THEY SAT STRANDED in the driveway of their new home. The garage door opened and they kept waiting long after its scratching and droning had stopped. He opened a window and then stopped moving again. He was not yet ready to squeeze past boxes and boxes toward the empty kitchen.

This is what we dreamt of, he said. Happy walls.

Yes, she agreed.

The evening was full of light and pretty. Full of golden light and exceedingly pretty. California. Wine country. They both had jobs.

They studied the boxes, their faces blank, their faces tired. Their faces were still young enough to be called young; it had taken them sixteen years to get here.

We're going to have a yard sale, she said.

I swear, he said, one day I'm setting it all on fire. The dog had spotted them from the window and started to bark. They had closed four days prior.

They kept sitting in the car. He opened a bottle of Kombucha from one of the grocery bags in the backseat and passed it to her. "It's local," she said. They had sold their house in a dusty part of the country people didn't know belonged to this country. They had liquidated their retirement funds. All they had to do now was to keep working for the next thirty years.

The sun behind them prepared to dip from view, sending a last long gaze from behind the backs of the houses surrounding Coffey Park. Their own house said a fond good-bye and blushed. Wherever you stood in this neighborhood, you could see at least two palm trees.

"We're just going to leave the garage door open," she said. "People will start taking things. Boxes will disappear. At first they'll take the bikes, the lawn mower. Then the wardrobes will be gone. They won't leave anything behind."

She still was carded at stores that sold wine and liquor. When asked about her profession, she still turned red with shyness and mumbled something about event planning. She worked from home, never bothered to get out of her yoga pants. Her hair was a flower. Often she didn't shower until evening.

She'd wanted to be a painter, she'd wanted to be a yoga teacher. She'd waited for him to get his career going. She'd fed and clothed him for many years, she'd waited patiently her turn. They were in California. Wine Country. They couldn't afford for her to stop working.

He still had the swagger of junior faculty eager to be the whiz kid, the one who won't stop publishing books and organizing writers' conferences after getting tenure. He flung a look back along the way he'd come. His path into and around academia had been crooked. After long years of teaching in towns and colleges nobody had ever heard of and whose names he needed to repeat at least twice, in states that were ranked in the bottom five in the categories that counted, he had finally made it. One of his books had been recognized.

He remembered the advice of a professor in graduate school. That old man had been very serious in laying down the law that no writer should get caught up in the politics of the university. If they came to make you chair, you had to refuse. If they wanted you to serve on Senate, refuse. Summer classes, refuse. Office hours, to hell with them. Well, here he was; he had volunteered for every available committee; he held more office hours than mandated. He was smart and quick and he would not exhaust himself. After years of working extra hours and extra weeks to build and fatten his resume, he would make these years his best years. Those old teachers were rather grouchy, some of them, he thought.

To keep up his looks he worked out three days and ran twenty-five miles a week. He was still full of promise, he was humming along. He was a newcomer in this land, and it was his first spring. He meditated upon his frailty as a creature of desk chairs and small print, and upon man's frailty in general, able only to live within certain narrow limits of habit and adventure; and from there on it led him to the conjectural field of immortality and man's place in the universe. He needed to read a good book. They lay in untidy stacks on his office desk, his chairs, the floor.

She lifted the receiver and listened to the squeaks and rattles and ups and downs of a human voice. The voice seemed to know her, the voice seemed familiar. She hung up mid-sentence, stared at the button-covered machine with wonder. A conference was approaching, she could see it announce its importance on her calendar. Maybe the voice had been connected to catering? Had it been her boss? She was still wearing her jammies. She poured lukewarm coffee over the phone, waited for a sign of its death.

He stood in front of twenty-two students. There was no explosion and no disaster. No blackout, no aneurysm. His words stopped coming. Whatever was in his brain didn't want to find its way out of his mouth. Nothing could be translated into sounds anymore. It was painless. He shut his mouth, without smiling and without sweating. He sat back down in his chair. He looked around.

What bothered them were the noises coming from the garage. At night, it woke the dog and the dog woke them with its sharp barks. Did you lock the door to the kitchen, he asked. Yes, she said, I made sure of it.

In the morning, coffee in hand, he surveyed what was left. To his surprise, the weed whacker remained in one corner. But several boxes had vanished overnight. Kitchen stuff, he thought. A trail of bungee cords went past the open garage door and down the driveway. Silly pictures of flowered gardens the seller's agent had left from the staging didn't lean against the wall anymore. The scavengers, he thought, were somehow still here. He meant to still feel their fingers rifling through bank statements of the last ten years, photo albums full of snap shots from ball games and weddings and road trips. All the faces ever showed were teeth. Nobody had yet touched his office and book boxes. His running shoes had stood below the deep plastic sink the night before.

They visited Wolf House, they visited the museum where an exhibit showed pictures and artifacts of Jack London's life. He had the right idea, he said. She nodded. Behind them a man in his sixties said, How much life he squeezed into his years!

They heard that same sentiment expressed again in the upstairs room, this time by a young woman with her three kids.

He read, Up to the last day of his life he was full of bold plans and boundless enthusiasm for the future.

We could be like Jack and Charmian, she said. We sell the house and buy a ship and set sail. We'll snark to Borneo, Java, and Shanghai.

He held her, their love for each other strong, their love for each other as safe and secure as their jobs. They were good at getting through days. They were so good at it. They seized them and got through.

During the week, she locked herself in the bedroom she had converted into an office. The dog roamed the yard and the house. The sliding door from kitchen to yard stood open all day, the garage door opener he had crushed with an old shovel nobody had bothered to carry off.

The dog was a Chinook, the proper sled-dog, tan-and-white coated and mellow. The animal was depressed by the move. It knew that it was no time for making a home. Its instinct told it a truer tale than was told to the man and woman by their judgment. The dog experienced a vague but menacing apprehension that subdued it and made it slink along the fence, and that made it question eagerly every unwonted movement of the world behind the fence. It ignored the scraping sounds coming from the garage and peered longingly up at the window behind which the woman was typing. He was in love with her; he did not dare whine.

In the evenings they drank Pinot Noir, at the far end of the backyard below the apple tree. They kept their voices low so as not to disturb the scavengers. They heard the floorboards creak, they heard the bathroom door squeal. From neighboring yards came the smells of barbeques, sounds of steps on cement, harsh words in raised voices. Darkness replaced light. He could feel his teeth turn purple. He stroked her hair, made love to her shoulder. Her skin was still white, still visible. They were warm, they didn't need any light or fire. Beams of flashlights played along their windows.

Did you lock the door? he asked later. The mattress was still theirs, too heavy and unwieldy to be removed by quick and silent fingers. Only our bedroom door, she whispered. Good, he said. He put his arm around her torso, a hand came to rest on her breast.

He couldn't read what was happening to him. Off the page, he was helpless, short-sighted. When it came to the matters of the soul – and how he hated the word 'soul' – he had no imagination. No intuition. He felt, but he couldn't translate those emotions which appeared to him as so many blankets; you got too warm and needed to throw them off.

He'd skipped every single committee meeting the last few weeks. During office hours he locked the door. He missed department meetings, he hadn't read or answered any of his emails. He hadn't written a single page of a single story. "You were right, old hoss; you were right," he mumbled. He held on to her.

The car stopped two miles before he had reached the house. When he had left in the morning, she had been quiet, her skin translucent. The anxiety seemed to have left her. A smile flared her lips. They sat on the floor of the empty living room. The carpets were gone, though some rubber mats reminded them of what had once been. The floor showed black footprints – it had rained one night a few nights back. They leaned against the walls in one corner, her feet in his lap. They drank coffee; she had moved the coffeemaker and two cups into the bedroom – like a hotel, she had said. They thought they heard the dog in the yard. Your hair is a flower, he said. She screwed up her eyes but didn't pat it down. He cracked her toes, massaged her feet. There was no radio left, no iPad, no phone. The birds were left in the apple tree, their song unaltered cheerful. Noisy really. How many birds are there? she asked. Just one? It must be several, he said. Or maybe it is only one, changing his tune.

After the mower was taken, the grass had enjoyed its new freedom and done its thing. Weeds grew in every crack of the paved way from front entrance to sidewalk. Other dogs had defecated in the driveway.

She put a hand over his, moved it lightly over his dry skin. Their fingers intertwined. They drank their coffee, her feet cold, a bit blue now.

He'd seen the yellow warning light come up on his way to the office. He'd done nothing about it, had parked his car in the general lot, taken the elevator to the third floor of his building and sat in his office for four hours, the door locked, his window cracked open. He'd still felt his wife's feet in his lap, and he'd looked out the window into the trees and fell asleep feeling nothing.

He walked the two miles home, forgetting he'd ever owned a car. He should have gotten rid of it so much earlier, he thought, then forgot that thought as well.

It wasn't burning anymore, the fire trucks had gone leaving behind a gray and black sludge. White wisps of smoke ascended unhurriedly from a few places. A neighbor came, a man he'd never seen before, whose name he'd never heard. That man wore running shoes that looked familiar. His words were a deluge, a white wall of sounds he could only run from. Where was she?

"You," he said when he was alone again, sweating from the effort. "April. Willow. Summer. Hemlock." Those were her names, weren't they? He sorted through what he knew of names, what names he knew and the right one eluded him still.

He rested against the fence, the ruined house in his sight, so that he might see her should she remember him. She would come, hold out her hand and he would take it and follow her. It was of no importance where they went, they just needed to go.

Then he drowsed off into what seemed to him the most comfortable and satisfying sleep he had ever known. The dog appeared from he didn't know where and sat facing him and waiting. The day drew to a close in a long, slow twilight. As the twilight drew on, the dog's eager yearning for food mastered it, and with a great lifting and shifting of forefeet, it whined softly, then flattened its ears down in anticipation of being chided by the man. But he remained silent. Later, the dog whined loudly. And still later it crept close to the man. The scent made the animal bristle and back away. A little longer it delayed, howling under the stars that leaped and danced and shone brightly in the sky. Then it turned and trotted up the street in the direction of the next subdivision, where there were other food-providers and bed-providers.

WANTS

STACY BIERLEIN

I SAW MY EX walking toward me on 26th Street. It seemed that he had come out of the coffee shop, but he had never liked coffee, the taste or the smell. Our paths met in front of Sweet Rose, the creamery that always had my daughter's favorite banana ice cream, although I doubted he would remember that now.

Hello life, I said. We had been together for years so I felt justified.

Life, he said tilting his head back as he chuckled. What life? No life of mine.

I didn't argue. I made efforts never to argue with him when there were too many words that could go badly; the possibilities for him to think I meant things I did not mean.

I was carrying a heavy canvas bag full of books, old poetry collections that had been the right poems at the wrong times. They had been stacked in the back of my hall closet for years. At first I was saving them for the kids, until one by one they were grown up and studying in New York and reading everything on devices. I decided I would sell these collections back to the bookstore at the country mart.

My ex followed me away from Sweet Rose, past a valet stand, through the faux barn door, and into the bookstore. I was thinking that I didn't understand how time passed. I'd had those books in my closet for years and the bookstore is only four blocks away.

My ex poked around for several minutes neither ignoring nor engaging. Finally he interrupted the bookstore associate who was trying to tell me the value of things.

In many ways, he said, as I think about it, I attribute the dissolution of our relationship to the fact that you never bothered to like my script.

I took a deep breath, shook my head. He was still talking about his damned spy screenplay, the one set in Beirut that had too little character development and never saw the light of day.

You kept wanting to rearrange scenes and verbs. You couldn't find the heart of it, the way you did with your poems, he said, pointing to the books spread out on the counter. You should have tried—really tried—to like it.

That's possible, I said. But really, if you remember, my Uncle Harold died that Friday afternoon; I had to drive back and forth from La Jolla. The kids were young and needed us so much. I taught those workshops, then the stock market crashed. We didn't share our writing much anymore. But you're right. I should have tried harder to like the script.

The bookstore associate pulled money out of a drawer and counted out forty-two dollars.

A nice thing I do remember is breakfast, he said.

I was surprised. We used to go to a French cafe on Montana Avenue that isn't there anymore. The *Mean Girls* actress and her German boyfriend always took the table next to us. I was usually a little mad at him in the morning. I had it in my head that healthy relationships had lots of morning sex. He was fidgety in the morning, anxious, unwilling to linger in bed. I had imagined the mean girl's guy was sexier, naughtier, accommodating.

We were fighting then, I said.

When were we ever not fighting? he said.

Oh, as time went on we didn't disagree as much. The kids gave us a lot to agree about, I reminded him. And we wanted to be our best for them. We tried to give them good childhoods and interesting opportunities. Some of the time it was really nice.

The bookstore associate smiled faintly as he inched further away from us. I thanked him in case I had forgotten before. It was delightfully simple, I thought, cash for books. No one handed you cash anymore; everything was a quick swipe, a chip and a click. Actually money was rarely in our hands, our needs always debited.

I wanted to make big films, he said, our kids wanted to travel. But you—you never wanted anything.

Clearly the things he was saying pleased him. And this part was true. He was always searching for a mighty plot. I kept stalling and striving to take care of sentences.

Don't be bitter, I said.

Then he said, with great bitterness, I have a new film in production you know. I have enough financing in place to take this one all the way. This one could go to the Academy Awards. This is the victory I've been waiting for and there will be more for me. It's all going swimmingly. But it's too late for you. You could've been doing the big things for years now, but you've never wanted it badly enough.

He had a habit throughout our years of making a shallow comment which, like a plumber's snake, could work its way through my ear down to my throat then jab again and again at my heart. He would suddenly disappear, leaving me choking on the equipment.

I told him I had forgotten something at the counter. I went in to purchase one of the poetry collections I had just sold back. It was the right time now. Marie Howe. *What the Living Do.* How we go on when too much is decided for us.

What I mean is, I turned for a moment to see him walking fast to his car. He pulled his old Prius out of its parking space, into traffic, further away, a blur in the distance.

I carried *Living* to the wrought iron bench outside Sweet Rose. I sat for a moment; I needed to keep my balance. I felt extremely accused.

Actually I had wanted things. Of course I had. I wanted to make art that spoke for us. I wanted to get through the tasks of the day.

I wanted to be two places at the same time, nurturing my curious, wild little children; and also traveling with him to Beirut so that he could get the rhythm of the city correctly onto the page instead of relying on the impressions of a director friend who once glimpsed it from the window of the Four Seasons.

I want, for instance, to be a different woman, to be the kind of woman who puts her old books back into circulation the very week she thinks of it. I want to be strong, to use my voice, to be an effective citizen. I want to be the kind of person who changes something, who rights a wrong in the court system, or addresses the politicians and calls out the assholes.

I want to cheer up.

I wanted to have been loyal forever to one person, the ex, or the man I met too quickly after him. Either had enough character and verve for a whole life, which now feels too short a time. I couldn't have exhausted either man's qualities or fought my way under the rock of their true reasons in just one piece of time, could I?

I *had* promised the children I would improve our personal economy.

I had wanted that morning sex, or at least his arm to reach out for me in the morning as if I had rolled too far away in the bed during the night.

I want to remember it all correctly.

Just this morning I looked out the window to the street and saw how the jacaranda tree had changed overnight. The flowers were in brilliant view now, each of them screaming varied shades of purple and blue, all of them precious, like fully realized little poems. A developer had planted the tree when my youngest was still in pull-ups and suddenly on this day it was in the prime of its life.

So I decided to take those books to the country mart. Which proves that when a person or event comes along to jolt me, I do take the appropriate action. I hear this traffic. I can feel the ache of people going away.

A swift breeze brings the scent of coffee this way again. The thing that gets to him is this: I am better known for really thinking things through. People know me for my quiet manner, and some crisp phrases.

Luna Beach

Jane Dykema

We'd lived on the island almost a year. Long enough for some shit to happen but not long enough to be from there. We didn't want to be from there, anyway. We were from Ponce, a real city where we had friends and things to do, where you'd see someone you didn't know once in a while. Mom moved us over from the main island for a better nursing job, which didn't mean more money just that she'd be in charge of people. If we hadn't moved, Dad wouldn't have started sleeping with the hostess at Rosie's Dockside Grill who was married to the owner, and then the owner wouldn't have stabbed Dad in the street outside Rosie's. Most people thought the hostess was Rosie, but Rosie must have been the owner's mom or first wife, because the name on the letters we found and that we never showed Mom said Clara.

After Dad died, either Mom's talking increased or we hadn't realized how much of it Dad had been absorbing. The talking didn't pause, and there was nowhere to go to escape. We lived in a tourist area, not knowing any better at first, at the end of a row of shops, in a dark, three-room place with a tin roof, a dirt road in front, a slope of trees in the back that eventually stopped at the canal. So when Ricky finally had it with the talking, he decided to build a tarp-shelter in the mangroves behind our house.

That's when Jimmy from Jimmy's Jeep Rental caught us stealing tarps from his lot. It turned out Jimmy didn't just conduct business out of the trailer beside his Jeep rental, he slept there, too. When he caught us it felt like the time my Puerto Rican History teacher caught me cheating on the midterm. But I hadn't been cheating; I checked my neighbor's test to see what question he was on, to see if I was falling behind and needed to speed up. I tend to fall behind. When I looked from his paper to Ms. Acevedo, her gaze hardened on me. She shook her head. I loved her. She called me Miss Mercado instead of Louisa. She took me seriously and her eye shadow always matched her blouse. I watched the way she saw me change, and I didn't have the courage to tell her it was a misunderstanding.

I loved Jimmy, too. He was especially nice to us after Dad died. Other people looked at us the way we look at the homeless, not disgusted but embarrassed and uncomfortable. Mom said a homeless person is like a mirror, reflecting back at us a version of ourselves who doesn't know what to do. But Jimmy called me Doc instead of Louisa and always stopped us to talk when we passed by on our way to school. The talks were so reliable and long-lasting we had to leave earlier and earlier to still make it on time, and I realized after learning about his cancer and his plans to buy a helicopter, that they were as much for him as for us.

The tarp situation differed from the test: we were doing what Jimmy thought we were doing, and he didn't seem disappointed. In fact, when the three of us stood in his lot in the hot middle of the night, one rooster calling, Ricky's shirt collar balled up in Jimmy's fist, it seemed like he liked us more. He said he wouldn't tell Mom if we hosed off the returned rental Jeeps for a month.

Jimmy rented Jeeps to tourists. The tourists, already sunburned from the two-hour ferry ride over from the main island, draped their arms over new hiking backpacks with shoes dangling off them. Their sunglasses stayed balanced on the brims of their hats while they nodded at Jimmy. Jimmy drew maps of all the roads on the island down to the soil composite of each, marked all the potholes with dots pressed so hard sometimes the paper tore. He had very specific instructions about which roads to avoid, instructions the tourists never followed, and so the Jeeps came back with mud up to the roof racks. I was grateful for the tourists not giving a shit because it meant Jimmy needed us.

Part of Jimmy's lecture to the tourists was never to go to Luna Beach. Sometimes the ocean current washed up drugs from boats running through the neighboring island onto Luna, so there were, from time to time, drugs and drug runners on that beach, which was secluded, barricaded from the rest of the island by a mile deep of protected wildlife refuge. Only accessible on foot, Jimmy said the hike was almost as dangerous as whatever might be on the beach.

Two of his customers didn't heed his warning, Jimmy told the tourists, and halfway through the refuge a couple of guys with machine guns appeared. Apparently, they let them run instead of killing them. Probably better for the smugglers to have rumors instead of tourist bodies.

Obviously, the first thing Ricky and I did when we overheard that part of Jimmy's speech was ride our bikes to the edge of the refuge and start hiking to Luna Beach.

At first the hike was fine, but hot. And we were like, what the fuck, this hike is normal. But then Ricky fell in a ditch, onto a rotting deer, who had also fallen into the ditch and apparently hadn't been able to get out. Ricky got out by standing on the deer and me pulling him up, lying on my stomach with my legs hooked on some trees.

I wanted to turn back, mostly because Ricky smelled like a rotting deer and it was the worst smell I'd ever smelled. It burned my eyes. I threw up. Ricky said to quit being a pussy— he was the one who fell and he wanted to keep going.

The space we could walk through got shallower and shallower; roots grew high out of the ground, and massive hives heavy with bees hung low out of every fourth tree.

We were high stepping, bent so low we couldn't see more than five feet ahead, and sweating like crazy.

"This is fucked-up," I said, and ran into Ricky who had stopped in a clearing to stretch his back.

We stood for a second to catch our breath.

Then we heard the rustling. From something big, getting louder. Headed right for us. We froze, waiting to get blown away by two guys with machine guns.

It was a horse. A wild horse on an island five miles by six miles. There were a few and this was one of them, as surprised to see us as we were to see it.

We didn't consult each other—we'd both pissed ourselves—just turned around and headed back to our bikes.

Ricky didn't like failing. Not only had we failed at tarp-shelter, we'd failed at the first, tarp-stealing step. And now this.

For two days Ricky walked in and out of our three rooms without saying anything. By not trying to talk to him, I showed him I was waiting.

"We've got to get a look at that beach," Ricky said, finally.

Drones were expensive, especially the kind with a two-mile range and that broadcast real-time footage to your phone you mount on the handset. Especially with the shipping it cost to get anything sent to an island off the coast of an island. So we asked Jimmy if we could keep hosing off the Jeeps for money after we paid our debt.

Honestly, we probably would have done it without the money—it was good to get out of the house since Mom had lost her goddamn mind. I didn't blame her, but it still wasn't easy to be around the talking. If you could die from being talked to, Ricky and I would have died a thousand deaths everyday. And we did, in a way. She didn't seem to be working out her feelings; she wasn't talking about Dad. She said, out loud, what she was doing, what we were doing, what she would do, all the things that could go wrong, everything she wondered, asked what she was forgetting, listed every possible thing it could be. She'd ask one of us a question and then guess at the answer until we walked away into one of the other two rooms.

Ricky and I took turns spending time in the bathroom. I don't know what he did in there. I stood and looked at myself in the mirror. Sometimes I thought I looked really pretty. I wished someone else were watching, that my chin or my hair at that moment, at that angle, would be witnessed, captured in someone else's memory. Sometimes I looked terrifying; I didn't make any sense to myself. That I existed, that the person I saw was me, I didn't know what that meant. Through the door, I'd hear Mom talking to Ricky. It built and built, seconds seemed like hours, and I could never leave him out there for long.

Jimmy gave us more than just hosing. He taught us how to change tires, change oil, diagnose a check engine light. He talked a lot, too, but his talking wasn't urgent and desperate like Mom's, demanding your attention like a sting, like irregular dripping you can't tune out. Jimmy's talking was like having the radio on.

Outside school, the hostess waited for us. I'd never seen her, and she didn't look how I expected, was older and weirder-looking than Mom, but I knew it was her. Sometimes you know something; it feels familiar even though it's never happened before.

She leaned against her long, dusty-blue car and when we got closer she stood and straightened her skirt.

"Do you know who I am?" she asked.

Ricky was startled, didn't realize anything was happening between us and this stranger till she spoke.

"No," he said aggressively, the way he says things when he's surprised.

"Clara?" I said.

She nodded, tears in her eyes. "I've seen your pictures," she said.

"What?" Ricky said.

He trained his gaze above her head, the way he did when pretending not to understand.

"I just wanted to tell you," she said, taking a step forward, "I loved your dad so much. I loved him so much."

"But you broke up with him," I said. I'd read the letter. I didn't mean it as an accusation. I didn't understand why you'd break up with someone if you loved them. A fan of love, I rooted for it even when it ruined my own family.

"I was trying to protect him."

"Good job," Ricky said.

She fell back against her car and cried. I thought one of us should hug her but I'm not good in an emergency. I looked up at Ricky. We both stood still, arms dangling.

"We should have been nicer," I said after she drove away, implicating myself, too, even though I meant Ricky.

"That fucker killed Dad," Ricky said.

I couldn't think of anything worse than having killed someone.

Jimmy always wore a baseball cap, gray frizz puffing out around the sides. When he lifted it off to readjust it in the heat, the hair kept its hat-on shape. His skin was the darkest it could naturally go from working outside everyday. He made us wear sunscreen but never put any on himself. "I don't worry about that stuff," he said. "Stress kills."

We handed him back all the money he'd handed us each week, a damp $800, and asked him to order us the Falcon 4-Stretch Quadcopter since we didn't have a credit card and didn't want to involve Mom.

He whistled, read the product details aloud.

"See all kinds of shit with this," he said.

Standing behind Jimmy, looking over him at the screen, Ricky smiled a real smile.

He practiced all the time. After school and before Mom got home we'd find a level spot of ground in the trees behind our house and Ricky would fly the drone and I'd watch. Sometimes I brought a book and laid it open in my lap but I always just watched. Sometimes Ricky asked if I wanted to try, less out of generosity and more because he would have more fun if I understood how hard it was, but I liked watching people do things more than doing them myself.

In the afternoon heat, he crashed the drone into the canopy over and over. Then he guided it up through the canopy a couple of times, then more and more. He improved quickly.

I shifted my weight from one side to the other, scratching at the indentations roots and sticks made on the backs of my thighs. Every day was hotter than the last. The leaves burst green, drooped. I could hear them being.

"Did you see that?" Ricky said.

He'd landed the Falcon perfectly on a stump.

"That was crazy," I said.

Ricky felt good working toward something. I felt good when he felt good.

One night it started raining and never stopped. Our first rainy season on the island. Rain thundered off the tin roofs. You couldn't hear anything else. Everyone, hoarse from yelling, became more selective about what they had to say. Except Mom.

One rooster in our neighborhood, confused, called all night. Between four and five in the morning the others joined, and soon it sounded like hundreds, a roaring stadium.

I'd get up before Ricky so he wouldn't make fun of me, huddle under the side awning, and spread out some feed. Four cats and seven chickens came out of nowhere, lined up to eat. No fights. I missed the city, but the country was growing on me. I didn't know whose the animals were yet. We'd been there a while, but not long enough to know everything everyone else knew. The smaller the community, the more there is to know.

When Ricky got up we went to the shop for milk and Coke. Normally in the wind the palm leaves sounded like clapping. Applause. But in the rainy season the leaves were so heavy and wet it was more like slapping. Everything turned sinister. Streets and fields flooded. The mangroves lining the canal twisted out of the water like fat frowns, roots submerged. They were beautiful.

We stopped on the red bridge to look at the mangroves, our bags from the shop slowly filling with water. Another thing that happens when it rains for that long is people stop giving a fuck. Like in war zones where there's gunfire and bombs going off and people are going to the store and to school like normal, we just walked around like it wasn't raining, didn't even duck under awnings because after a certain point, you can't get any wetter.

Mist hung around the trees, the red flowers like little fires. The rain dribbled metallic on the water. It was hot even in the rain, our bodies hot and wet on the inside and the outside.

"Fuck this." Ricky said. "We're doing it today."

Rain made Ricky restless. I was nervous what this kind of rain would do.

"We can't. It can't fly in the rain."

"It'll fly. We just have to get closer."

I didn't think he was right and I didn't want to get closer.

"It specifically says not to fly it in the rain," I said.

"It will never stop raining," Ricky said.

That seemed possible.

Dogfucker came around the corner with a bag from the shop, too. He wore shorts and black socks pulled up mid-calf. I moved over so he could pass us on the bridge. Ricky didn't.

"Wet enough for you?" Dogfucker said, squeezing around Ricky.

"Where's your dog?" I said.

"She doesn't like the rain."

We watched his bald head bob away, no hat, as if the sun were out.

"He totally fucks his dog," Ricky said.

"He seems nice."

"You can just tell," Ricky said, watching him. "Listen,

we'll tell Jimmy we're both sick and after Mom goes to work we're doing it."

"We're both sick?"

"Who cares?"

"What will we tell Mom when we die?"

"Fuck Mom."

He was right. Mom was an asshole. Well, not an asshole, exactly. She was imprecise with her energies. Dad, before he got stabbed, was very precise with his energies.

"We have to see what's over there."

The thing about Ricky was his thoughts weren't usually right, but he was right to think them. Sometimes I wondered if that was a patronizing way to feel. I thought about telling him, letting my honesty be the ultimate sign of respect, but I didn't think he'd see it that way.

Ricky made a show of groaning in the bathroom for a long time—I just acted normal—and after Mom went to work, we rode our bikes to the edge of the refuge, me shouting up at Ricky reasons for waiting.

"How do we know there are even drug runners there today?" I said.

"That drone cost $800," I said.

Rain was getting in my mouth. I could barely see.

"Okay," Ricky said when we stopped. He already had the drone out of his backpack, was snapping his phone into the handset. We huddled under some trees and tested it out.

It flew.

"The picture's okay," Ricky said.

And then, uncharacteristically, he looked at me to approve the decision.

Seeing him want my approval made me want to give it. I was all in.

"Let's do it," I said.

The drone lifted up, silently, and flew out over the trees toward the beach.

I stood behind him, looking over his shoulder at the screen in his hands. I'd never seen the tops of trees so close. The picture wasn't great because of the rain, but the leaves shone, water reflecting light when they shifted under the weight of more rain. I wanted to tell Ricky to hover around the trees longer but I didn't want to see his face after I asked.

It didn't take long to get to the beach. The whole plan was working. We could see pretty well, the sand darkened by rain, the white edges of the water, the way the beach looks when it's alone, all from the safety of perching two miles away with our bikes between our legs.

And then we saw it: two figures digging.

"Holy shit," I said.

"I'm going to get closer," Ricky said.

He was unsurprised, ready.

The men came into focus; one had his head covered and the other didn't. They took turns pitching their shovels in and heaving sand out.

We were both right: this was the day, and the drone wouldn't fly in the rain. Ricky lost the signal, lost control, and the camera stayed on. We watched the beach get closer and closer till our view crashed into the sand ten feet from the men. The image shifted with their footsteps and one of them picked up the drone, turned it over and looked straight into the camera.

Eyes like ice planets, a hairless head, and then the picture cut out.

Sitting on our front steps, we went over the possibilities. Could the drug traffickers use the drone to find us somehow if they had half and we had half? They knew someone had footage of their digging and ice-planet-face. How would they kill us?

Dogfucker came by with his dog, walking slowly. Even his dog didn't seem to notice the rain anymore.

"You got her out in the rain," I said.

"I wish it were under better circumstances."

Ricky sighed to show that he knew Dogfucker was going to keep talking to us and he didn't want him to.

"My cousin's dog died."

"Oh, no," I said.

"Cancer. He fought hard and lost, the way we're all going to go."

Sometimes people have to tell you something bad, and then tell you what they've learned from it to make the bad thing seem valuable, too.

"We could give the handset to Dogfucker," Ricky said after he left.

"We could throw it in the canal," I said.

Ricky stood up and walked in a big circle. He walked down the block till I couldn't see him anymore. I rested my chin between my knees and let the rain drum between my shoulder blades, rush off the tips of my hair.

When Ricky came back I said, "Look, we don't know enough to know what to be afraid of. We don't know how the drone works. We don't know how drug traffickers work. I think we should go tell Jimmy."

"No way."

"Jimmy will know what to do."

Ricky walked behind me the whole way to maintain his protest. For a second I couldn't tell if it was raining or it wasn't. It was.

We found Jimmy in the garage under a Jeep. It smelled wet and oily and I felt safe being there, anonymous. A few years before on the main island a man followed me out of the park when I left to go home. So instead of going home I ran into the supermarket, wove through all the isles and people until I was sure he was gone. Mom said that was exactly the right thing to do. Never lead them to where you live.

"These brake discs are fucked," Jimmy said when we got close enough to hear. He didn't roll out to see who we were. "I don't know what else to do aside from drive them around myself," he said.

"Oh. Ricky. Doc." He stood up. "You two look like you feel fine."

I wondered who he thought he was talking to if not us. He wore an expression I'd never seen. Nervousness. Or maybe anger that we'd lied about being sick.

On the way over I'd practiced how to explain the drone to Jimmy so we seemed as innocent as possible. We just happened to be flying it around, not looking for anything in particular. We certainly hadn't worked for him to save up for it and then had him buy it for us for the sole purpose of disobeying him. Only after we saw the traffickers did we remember his warnings about Luna. We were just kids. We were sorry. Did he think the traffickers would find and kill us? What should we do? But it all seemed so obvious when I opened my mouth to start. The twists and turns

I wanted to hide behind disappeared before I could put words to them and I just stood, unable to speak.

I looked for Ricky to see if he would help. He leaned against a long, dusty-blue car, trying to look uninterested.

I'd never seen a car other than a Jeep in the shop. I knew that car. It was the hostess's car.

Jimmy looked from me to Ricky with a weird energy, the way you do when you want someone to stay focused on you and not what you're hiding.

"What's this?" I pointed at the car.

"That?" he said, as if a meteor would land on us between that sentence and the next so he wouldn't have to continue. "Just tuning it up as a favor."

"You never work on anything but Jeeps," I said.

"Sure, sometimes."

I went over to the door, out into the rain, rounded the corner and saw a light on in Jimmy's trailer, a silhouette moving around the sink.

If Clara loved Jimmy, too, her love for Dad wasn't special. You can't just love everybody. I wiped my eyes. In the garage, Ricky still leaned against the car reading his phone like an idiot. I hated them both. Ricky for not seeing. Jimmy for being like Dad. For letting me find out and giving me power over him. For putting himself in danger, too.

"Listen, I'm about to head over to a little ceremony," Jimmy said. "You kids want to come?"

Jimmy patted his pockets, starting at the top of his vest and finally finding what he wanted in the cargo part of his shorts—a bottle of eye drops. He tipped back and squeezed 20 drops into each eye.

When we realized we were going to Luna, Ricky and I looked at each other as if we'd woken up in the same nightmare. We stayed quiet and kept going, not knowing what else to do. The hike was different this time. For one thing, it was pouring. And we were focused on keeping up with Jimmy instead of our own misery. The deer, mostly fur, still lay in the ditch.

We broke out onto the edge of the world, the beach unfamiliar but safe in the way you're safe when you're alone. Smooth, empty sand stretched toward a small crowd at the far end, everything gray and soft, like breathing. I couldn't tell what was sweat and what was rain.

As we got closer to the people huddled at the end of the beach, I recognized Dogfucker. He stood with his dog talking to another bald man, and when he turned I saw it was the man with ice planet eyes we'd seen through the drone.

"Oh my god," I said to Ricky, and tried to get him to slow down.

I pointed. Ice Planets had our drone in his hand, motioned around in the air with it, reenacted its landing for Dogfucker. The other digger was there, too. He stood looking into the hole they'd dug with two other mourners.

And then I realized they'd been digging not to cover or uncover drugs; they'd been digging a grave.

"It's a dog funeral," I said.

Usually when Ricky was wrong I didn't draw attention to it, in fact, I did the opposite, pretended not to notice his wrongness, pretended not to notice the whole situation leading up to his wrongness. What traffickers? What beach? Or even better, I narrated an alternate world that made more sense than ours in which he was right, Luna Beach was perfect for trafficking. If drug traffickers knew what they were doing they'd be here all the time.

But this seemed like a special circumstance. I didn't understand anything. I hated everyone.

"It's a dog funeral," I said again, and Ricky looked at me like I shouldn't test him.

"It's a dog funeral," I said and pushed him.

It only took seconds for Ricky to pin me, for my mouth to fill with wet sand, and, despite everything, I believed it was an accident, that he was just trying to subdue me and not hurt me when he leaned all his weight into the sharp edge of his forearm which was dug into my nipple. I screamed.

Jimmy dragged him off me, pushed him toward the water. He tried to help me up but I didn't want his help.

"What the hell?" Jimmy said.

"Where are the drug traffickers?" Ricky shouted at Jimmy.

"What's that?"

I sat in the sand and watched Ricky reveal that he cared about something. He breathed heavily, looked like a little kid.

"No, no, that's just to keep tourists out of here." Jimmy blinked over and over. "Don't ever travel, you two. We are the worst versions of ourselves when we travel."

I stood and brushed off my clothes, discretely rubbed my chest. I wouldn't look at Ricky. Or Jimmy.

No one seemed to notice or care that we fought. Dogfucker stood next to his cousin during the service, two bald heads slick with rain.

Ice Planets cried in the kind of ugly, uncontrollable way I saw Dad cry, the only time I saw him cry, when he read Clara's break-up letter the day before he died.

"He was a beautiful dog," Dogfucker said, because Ice Planets couldn't speak. "Chest as broad as the day is long."

Ricky elbowed me.

I hoped Ricky was right about Dogfucker fucking dogs. We needed to be right about something.

Craigslist Missed Connections

(The Life You Save May Be Your Own)

Alexander Lumans

The Heart of a Tramp — w4m

THE VERY FIRST THING I NOTICED about you was not that you were a tramp. And it was not that you were a harmless tramp. And it was certainly not your black tramp town suit or your brown tramp felt hat turned up in the front or your tin tramp tool box you carried by the handle. No. I noticed none of those elements integral to your tramp persona. What I first noticed about you was what wasn't there: your left arm. Or rather, what was only half there, your left coat sleeve folded up to the elbow. I wanted to ask you what happened. But I couldn't.

You see: I'm deaf. And I've never said a word in my entire life. But I can read lips better than anyone suspects.

When you first sauntered up to our fenceline, I sat on the porch wearing a short blue organdy dress you appraised with your clay-colored eyes. You offered me a square of gum. Its flavor vanished as soon as I popped it into my mouth. This is the disappearing way of the world.

Absences have always fascinated me. Thunder, holes, sleep. Do they capture you? If my mother, who was sitting on the porch next to me when you approached, hadn't been present, I would have passed my hand through the space where your left forearm should have been; instead, I stamped and pointed and produced noises because that's what my mother expects of me. Do you believe in ghosts? Do you believe in love? Do you think there is a difference? You said that a doctor in Atlanta had taken a knife and cut out of a man's chest a human heart— *the human heart*—the doctor held it in his hand, studying it like day-old chicken, that's what you said, and then you said that he, the doctor, "don't know more about it than you or me." You were talking to my mother, but I like to think you were secretly talking to me, through the spaces between the words, telling me that you did know something of the human heart. My heart that is human.

I must tell you: I had the distinct urge to allow you to cut out my own heart, hold it up to the sunset's dimming light, and tell me that it had lain empty for too long. Because it has. I am thirty years old and all I know is this farmstead: its water pump by the house corner, its three or four chickens, its decrepit shed with a car that hasn't run in fifteen years. I would have run away already if I thought I'd find that other life on the far side of those three mountains; justified, I am, in dreams.

You said the world was almost rotten—*Almost*—and in the same breath you said your name was Mr. Tom T. Shiftlet. You said you might be named Aaron Sparks from Singleberry, Georgia, or George Speeds from Lucy, Alabama, or Thompson Bright from Toolafalls, Mississippi. This made me desire you more. The fact that I could not pin you down. That your insurmountable shadow was a thing I could bloom inside. You have not yet asked my name.

Please don't leave. We've only acquainted ourselves. And I am afraid of you.

Reply with what happened to your arm so I'll know it's really you.

Fifteen Min. Later, Tramp on the Porch — w4m

You rolled your own cigarette, and afterward, you did a thing I have never seen before: you struck the wooden match on the bottom of your shoe. *And it lit!*

You: magician. You: firestormer. You: significantly soulless.

You watched it dance there like it was a mystery you were trying to master while it burned down toward your fingers. I shook my finger at you; I didn't know what I was doing. I have watched different birds fall completely out of the sky because they flew too high. Finches, blues, once a hawk. Laugh if you'd like. It's not that the birds flew to a heaven where they weren't wanted by the Lord, if the Lord is something you believe in; it was simply the fact that they weren't prepared for the rarified air of a stratospheric ascent. That is where we differ.

You asked my mother what a man was, and then you said you were a carpenter, as if there were a link between the two. Also, you provided a list of all that you had been, none of which impressed me, though they were accolades all the same (gospel singer, undertaker, wrangler); only when you mentioned that you had "fought and bled in the Arm Service" did I take notice of your history from my spot between the swing and my mother's rocking chair.

Did you mean to say "Arm" and not "Armed" Service? Was that a joke? You are almost a funny man. Would you hold it against me if I said that at that exact moment I could feel the invisible fingers of your missing hand running through my hair? And that they smelled of peppermint and cordite? That fat yellow moon illuminated my mother striding up to you, asking, "Are you married or are you single?" I was too distracted by your phantom hand squeezing the back of my neck to hear your response. But the hot hand of anger suddenly gripped me right where yours had been because I realized what my mother was doing: she had taken measure of you and found it suiting herself, the same way a snake lies down next to its prey to see if it will fit in its long belly.

I draped my hair over my face. I covered my ears. I fell over and pretended to weep.

I could tell you and her were discussing what to do with me because when you cannot hear and you cannot read lips, you pick up on everything else. The way a tramp pivots his feet. The way a mother cocks her hip. The secrets that kicked gravel tells. There is a fire in grief. And I've lost everything I've never had. Show me again how to set the air aflame with just a wave of your hand.

When I finally brought myself to look up at you in that caustic moonlight, you were claiming you could fix everything on our farm—"one-arm jackleg or not. I'm a man even if I ain't a whole one...."—you reached down and rapped your knuckles against the porch boards as if you were testing their state of brokenness. "...I got a moral intelligence." You surprised yourself with this proclamation, I could tell, but you embraced it, like swelling into the coat of someone larger. How our porch was involved with where your ethical compass pointed, I did not know. But any man who claims he is a good man is asking for the opportunity to prove himself wrong.

My name is Lucynell. My mother told you this. It is her name too. A namesake will never admit this, but a damage dogs the footsteps of the patently crooked. To put it elsewise: my mother is not good enough for you and you are not enough for my mother. I am even less sure you should stay because I want you to take me away with you.

Reply with the last thing you said to my mother about monks so I'll know it's really you.

Am I Alive or Just Breathing? — w4m

You've been sleeping for almost a week in the Ford. Shave with a razor and a can of water, all in the mirror you propped on the rear windshield. You hung your coat on a hook in the backseat. While you've been fixing the garden shed roof and the flimsy gutters and the hole in the clapboards that lets in the winter, I've been making faerie crowns.

The faerie crown is exactly what it is. That's why it's a miracle, if you believe in things like angels and life after death. When I wear a crown, it makes me queen of the faeries, even though I have forgotten where all the faeries went. This sounds childish, I admit, but everyone has a choice to be loved or to be free, and until I saw you and your missing arm, I thought I most wanted to be free. But a queen is never free, as an illusion, until it is burning, is never real enough to hold in your hand.

To make a faerie crown: first take a resilient vine or branch and tie it into a circle. Zigzag it against itself. Tighten it until it is a line ready to be plucked or cut; this is the easiest part. The most difficult is choosing the flowers for a crown because a crown is not arbitrary jewels thrown into molten gold; just as a doctor holds up the human heart to examine it for imperfections and biological verities, I hold up flowers to estimate their staying power, their ecological acquiescence.

A lily does not answer to a tulip. A dandelion will have any old idea. A sunflower wants to be the center of attention and is too heavy to be anything but. I used to think that flowers could talk to me, the way they talked to John Muir. But when I was twelve I realized I was speaking for them, throwing my mind's voice into their violet stamens. Still, I crafted crowns the way you said a mechanic crafted a car: a hundred men making one thing meant no one cared enough, but one man making one car meant he put all his love—*almost his whole heart*—into that one thing.

I knew I was most beautiful in the nighttime, with a faerie crown snapped to my nest of hair, the white bulbs glowing like headlights. I want you to think so too. Because I have always thought there's a better life on the other side, wherever the faeries have gone, that side, that double life.

Reply with the word that you taught me to say so I'll know it's really you.

Bird in Search of a Cage — w4m

The day I gave you a faerie crown of sunflowers and ivy, you taught me the word "bird."

The crown, I wanted to say, could keep the unforgiving sunlight out of your river-bottom eyes. You took it from my fat fingers. You looked at it like you were determining whether something fundamental was missing. Then you said that my mother had told you that she "wouldn't give me up for a casket of jewels." A trick, I knew. This was my mother's way of taking you for herself, without you knowing it. When you told me that, I felt invisible in the afternoon. As if I were made of less light than the day itself and therefore washed out by the open rays. If jewels grew on low-hanging branches or sprouted in the flowerbed, I'd make a casket of jewels for you and me to sleep in, just like the monks, rather than the Ford's cracking backseat. This is what I will think about tonight when I go to sleep in my dark room and touch myself twice under the dead-cotton sheets.

I followed you everywhere, repeating what you taught me: "Burrttddt, ddbirrrttdt."

I clapped my hands each time. "Burrttddt!" and I pointed at the crows in the cottonwood across the road. I clapped for you to teach me more words. "Teach me how to say 'effervescent' and 'champagne' and 'synergy'!"—I desperately craved to tell you this, but you took my singular applause as evidence that I was happy with what I already had. I would not tell you that when I pictured your missing arm, I pictured one smoke-grey wing sprouting in its place.

As I followed you in and out of the shed, the yard, the garden, begging for more, I could feel my mother's eyes steeled on me, secretly pleased with herself. The more exasperating I became, the more you would want her instead.

Do not want her. Do not.

Reply with the original color of the Ford so I'll know it's really you.

A Queen for a Prince — w4m

You, Mr. Arm Service, were fixing our impossible car because you had taken personal interest. I know nothing of automobiles. There is more of the world in the yolk of a robin's egg than on all the highways of this piebald country. A tramp like you might think otherwise.

"Ddbirrrttdt," I told you in earnest, by which I meant, "The heart cannot see the strings attached to it."

You shooed me away in fly-off fashion.

I made you faerie crowns every single day. You hung them from the rearview mirror instead of wearing them. In the slanted sunlight, they browned as quickly as I made them, as if hands rotted all that they touched. Plants, dreams, graves. I remembered you saying your first night here that the world was *almost* rotten, and I wondered if you were already a member of the rotted part or if you'd somehow escaped to our home. You said something about faeries belonging to a girl's world, and I realized you took me for a hopeless and sun-drenched dreamer rather than a Queen of Deliverance. Quietly and contentedly, you worked on our Ford until the planets came out in the dark blue sky and then sometimes you worked past that time. I wanted you to work on me instead. Come out of the yard darkness into the deeper darkness of my room and reveal to me the wonders of the other life available inside this one.

Reply with what color my eyes are so I'll know it's really you.

Something Special — w4m

There was one moment where I thought we had made progress toward my desires.

You were leaning into the open maw of the automobile's rust-caked hood, you were tooling around some unseen depth of a machine that has forever vexed me. I came around the car's side, said my one word. You lurched up, smacked your head against the inside of the hood, fell back in the grass. Your body scribbled up in a ball—I was afraid you'd knocked yourself out of the possibility of ever taking up with me. When you saw whom it was, you, holding the tenderized pate of your skull curtained on either side by flat black hair greased over with the sweat of the day, said, "I should have taught you to say 'Watch out' instead."

I said the word again, my way of apologizing, which you seemed to understand for the first time in our entire correspondence.

You asked, "You want to see something special?"

Even though my mother was out on the porch, unnerved and watching us, I knew she wouldn't be able to see whatever you were about to show me. I had my inklings. My seed of needs.

You took my hand, my hand as big as your hand, bigger even, so much so that mine could have easily encompassed yours. Together, like this, we leaned inside the Ford's open hood. It smelled of bird nests and old bonfires. You pointed out the parts of an automobile engine: pistons, carburetor, spark plug. You kept my hand in yours and then pointed my fingers at each thing you labeled. I felt as if you were in the process of naming the world, as if these things did not have names until you assigned them, as if you were a man of grand nomenclature who could mold the very mountain ranges as he saw fit.

"...And this is the brake line," indicating a black hose deep in the Ford's guts. "One of the most important features of a car. Cut that line? You're punching someone's one-way ticket."

Had I the voice, I would have told you that a one-way ticket was exactly what I wanted. Instead, I grazed the hose with our hands. Warm. I imagined it was you, your member, and I ran my finger down its tarry length until you shivered with an unseen—not unknown—thought.

Reply with what you were thinking about doing to me so I'll know it's really you.

Stupid Mandates of the Heart — w4m

You had walked into town to buy parts, paint, and gas. I sat on a chicken crate and waited all day for you. When you did not return, I stamped and screamed. "Burrddttt! Bddurrddtttt!" I knew you were gone then. You had made your decision about my mother and, more silently, you had made your decision about me—both of us: too empty, too unlit. I tore all the faerie crowns from the Ford's rearview. I burned them in the yard. I buried the ashes in a mass grave of blackened petals and curled stems. I turned toward the house with my mother rocking on the porch, and I imagined it all going up in a selfsame conflagration, lightning-wrenched, a trial by weather. What would we lose, honestly? All your repairs, yes, but I wanted no reminders of your overhauling influence. I wrote your name in ash and then wiped it away with a stick. Our wishes are shadows, tied gossamer thin to the legs of birds.

Reply with why you never returned so I'll know it's really you.

From Ashes to Autumn — w4m

Before sunset, you came whistling through the fence gate, as if I had called you into existence by erasing your name.

Within an hour, you had the Ford blasting alive in the shed. Then you backed it out of the double doors in a fierce and stately way, steering over the flowerbed. Your driving body: as stiff as the dead. Your expression: a cat's modesty— not a tramp's smirk—that belied the fact you had just raised the dead. The car's backend coughed black smoke, through which you pulled the machine, a body moving through ghosts of itself. In the turning of those ancient rubber wheels I saw my escape emerge from the cloud of unknowing and take shape. What I saw was myself in the passenger's seat and your left arm hanging out the breezed-by window.

That night, rocking on the porch, my mother asked if you wanted an innocent woman, claiming before you could answer that you did not want "none of this trash." I loathe the way she speaks: like a fallen angel with rocks in her mouth.

You said you did not—I didn't know if you meant innocence or trash.

Then my mother surprised me; she said that you wanted a girl who "can't talk," who "can't sass you back or use foul language."

"That's right," you said. "She wouldn't give me any trouble."

"Saturday," my mother said, "you and her and me can drive into town and get married." It sounded like she wanted all three of us to join together in matrimonial nesting. I could not determine what her sleight was, but I did not fancy it in the least.

You said you couldn't get married because you didn't have any money.

All our money was hidden inside a broken lockbox in a broken refrigerator out behind the house under an ivy veil. I knew you thought it was sewn up in the mattress, but that's where everyone hides their money, which makes it a hiding place no more. I was prepared to go fetch it, along with a long knife from the kitchen, so that my mother couldn't stop us.

Then you told her as much as you told me: "I wouldn't marry no woman that I couldn't take on a trip like she was somebody. I mean take her to a hotel and treat her." Those clay-colored eyes looked like they were about to stream tears of black gold.

135

"Lucynell doesn't even know what a hotel is."

I almost threw the chicken crate at her in the rocking chair; instead, I broke in half the faerie crown I'd been making for you to replace all the ones I'd burned, though I am unsure if you noticed them missing or the scorch mark in the yard. Goldenrod and cornsilk and bright white baby's breath: the recipe for apologies.

My mother said, "You'd be getting a permanent house and a deep well and the most innocent girl in the world. You don't need no money."

While you rolled yourself a cigarette and lit it in the same magical way, I was arriving at the realization that my mother had never had eyes on you. She was not that snake sizing up its to-be-devoured prey; she was measuring you down as suitable or not for her only child.

I cradled the halves of the faerie crown. I offered them to her but she refused the gift.

You fell back on philosophizing: "A man is divided into two parts, body and spirit. The body is like a house: it don't go anywhere; but the spirit is like a automobile: always on the move, always...." I wondered where the heart most resided: the body or the spirit. And what did that one doctor discover? Did someone love you once? Did someone cut out your spirit too? What is worse: that which we fail to experience or that which we regret having experienced? While I stepped into this river of thought, you and my mother negotiated how much she would give you for a weekend trip: just the two of us.

"I got to follow where my spirit says to go." You said this, as if you were reading the very contoured lines of my own buoyant spirit. I went and put my hand on the car's hood, felt its sun-stilled warmth, like a body's. It would, I knew, ferry us to another life.

Reply with how much money my mother finally offered you so I'll know it's really you.

I'm a Prize and I Want You to Unwrap Me — w4m

We were already on the road in the Ford you painted dark green with a yellow band around it just under the windows. It looked like a flower I knew no name for, it looked like a reflection of itself. I wore a white dress uprooted from my mother's trunk and a Panama hat with a bunch of red wooden berries in a spray around the brim like a queen's circle of rubies. I felt like the prize my mother called me before we left.

The day before, we'd married in the Ordinary's office in town. You weren't satisfied in the least: "If they was to take my heart and cut it out, they wouldn't know a thing about me." I've never seen lips pronounce truer words. I would gladly cut out your heart, hold it in my hand, read its truths and consequences.

I had almost forgotten you did not have both full arms, that's how familiar you'd become. But watching you drive, your one hand at the top of the wheel like you were holding your world in place, brought your missing part into stark relief. I wanted you even more. Every time you went to adjust the mirror, you asked me to hold the wheel. I knew then we were molded of one spiritual mode.

We were headed to Mobile. The sky: open, blue. The car: thirty miles per hour maximum. I thought of my mother and how she'd grabbed the sleeve of my dress after I'd climbed into the Ford. I had no intention of ever coming back, but I did not—could not—tell her. I'd looked straight through her to the house that would one day collapse under its own fear before the march of stormy flames, and then, as if I could feel what your arm wanted, you put the car in gear so that she had to let go of me.

Reply with what my mother called me as we drove away so I'll know it's really you.

A Wolf in the Throne Room — w4m

You kept up a heavy sighing, but you rarely spoke, so I had no idea what you were thinking while driving. Watching those motionless lips was as good as watching you speak in the dark, which I hoped would happen that night in Mobile, all before you removed my clothes layer by layer and officially took me as your wife. One hundred miles into the drive, I'd already plucked off every berry from my hat and flicked them out the open window. I kept thinking about your spirit, how much it wanted to be on the move, always. I knew you would leave me in Mobile. Or before it. At some point, your spirit would drag your heart away with it.

Reply with the name of the eating place we stopped at so I'll know it's really you.

Abandoned Angel of Gawd — w4?

I am alone. I am alone in this eating place, the Hot Spot. I am alone in the Hot Spot, knowing nothing except how much my heart weighs. As heavy as a faerie crown, as black as ash, as dead as a bird having hit the window, thinking it free air.

As I said before, I knew you would leave me. A good man always proves himself wrong, and a harmless tramp always proves himself right.

When we first pulled into the Hot Spot, I pictured us sitting down to eat on those counter stools with cushions the size of birdcage bottoms and having the most lavish meal of our two little lives and staying there until the very angels kicked us out of our own personal heaven. And then I just saw me: my arms cradling my head down on the counter, and you... you weren't anywhere in the picture. That life on the other side—the one I so desperately wanted to escape to? It's the same life, I realized, as the one on this side, only it cannot be saved. Nothing can. And neither would you.

After we sat down at the diner counter, you ordered me a large plate of ham and grits. The boy behind the counter, this young bird with a grease rag thrown over his shoulder, placed a knife and a fork and a napkin in front of me. He asked if I wanted any coffee. I shook my head, my bare hat falling to the checkerboard tile, my head feeling light and my thoughts wandering to the shadows. Meanwhile, you retired to the men's room. I thought better of the moment, or the moments to come, and what would be missing from them. I motioned for the boy. "Coffee?" he asked, and I shook my head again. Pointing to the car and saying "Bburrdddtt," I convinced him to follow me.

Outside, I rapped my knuckles on the Ford's hood. The boy, confused, lifted it. He looked at me like I was that prize my mother warned me I was.

With knife in hand, the one I filched from the counter, I leaned deep into the hood's shadow. I found that telltale black hose with its tarry ridges. And I gouged it open—not severed completely, but enough to see its brassy fluid start to ooze out. Afterward, I dropped the hood.

I wiped my hands on the boy's shoulder rag. He asked me what I was doing, and I pointed to my heart with the knife tip, pretending to cut it out.

I prayed that once you left me at the Hot Spot, you would not pick up a hitchhiker. Say, a boy with a small cardboard suitcase and a hat tilted away from where he'd come. Best case scenario: the clouds turned the shape of turnips and the color of the bags under your river-bottom eyes, these changes followed soon by a peal of thunder and fantastic raindrops; you pressed down that accelerator pedal, you stuck your stump out the window to feel a singular tingle in what wasn't there, and you raced the front of that storm until you came to the sharpest turn in the road.

Before you returned from the men's room, I arranged myself on the stool. Before my ham and grits were dished up, I laid my head down on the counter and closed my eyes. Before you walked out the Hot Spot's front door, I pretended I was asleep and I felt the boy staring at my pink-gold hair as he called me an "Angel of Gawd" and I heard you tell the boy that you'd pay for the food now because she—*me*—was a hitchhiker who was almost—*Almost*—home.

Reply with what kind of flowers I will place on your grave.

Reply with what kind of birds are singing the day your life ends.

Reply with what kind of road sign you saw before the world's rottenness engulfed you.

So I'll know it's really you.

OF THE REVOLUTION

BROCK CLARKE

THE LAST TIME I SAW MY FATHER was on Monument Square.
It was a Friday. I was thirteen years old. My school and my
father's office were within walking distance of the square, and
so every Friday afternoon at four we met there in front of the
monument and then walked to one of the nearby restaurants,
where he had a martini and I had a soda and we talked and
drank until my mother joined us there for dinner. I was a few
minutes early that day, and since I was standing in front of
the monument with nothing better to do, I decided to read
the plaque on its base. I'd stood there next to the monument
dozens of times, but had never bothered to find out who it was
supposed to memorialize: it could have memorialized a guy
named Monument for all I knew. But it didn't: the plaque said
it memorialized George Washington, whom the plaque called
"the Father of the Revolution."

I should mention that my father and I had been talking a
lot those days about what I was going to be when I grew up.
Except he'd never put it that way, exactly. Instead he'd kept
saying, "I worry about what's going to happen to you, Charlie.
I worry about it so much." He said this in the morning before
we both left the house. He said it at night as I was in bed,

waiting for him to say goodnight to me and to turn off the light. He said it at random times, on random days. He said it before he and my mother had their fights, and after them, and sometimes in the middle of them, too: I'd be upstairs in my room, trying to read or trying to sleep, and I'd hear their angry whispered back and forths from downstairs in the kitchen (they always seemed to argue in the kitchen) and in the middle of it my father would cry out, "But I worry about what's going to happen to Charlie! I worry about him so much!" Anyway, this had gone on for months and months, and so the subject—what was going to happen to me, what I was going to be when I grew up—must have been on my mind when I was standing there, in front of the monument of the father of the revolution. Because when my father came up behind me and asked, "Hey, what are you thinking?" I said, "I was thinking about how I'd like to be the father of the revolution when I grow up."

My father made a hissing sound between his teeth and said that probably wasn't such a hot idea.

"Why not?" I asked, and turned to face him. It was February, and there was a good bit of snow in my father's gray hair and on the shoulders of his black overcoat, too, even though it wasn't snowing that hard, and besides, my father's office was right across the square from where we were standing. It made it seem like he hadn't come straight from work, like he'd been walking around for a while. His face looked red and chapped and smelled like wet wool and cigarettes, even though, as far as I knew, my father didn't smoke. I expected him to gently whack me on the shoulder and say, "Hey bud" like he always did on Fridays when we met in the Square. But he didn't. He just stood there, a foot away from me, and looked at me gravely, as though he were seriously considering why I shouldn't, or couldn't, be the father of the revolution when I grew up.

"Because," my father said, hooking in his thumb in the direction of the monument. "There's already a father of the revolution."

"But if there weren't," I said.

"But there is," my father said. "And besides, I bet the father of the revolution would be a little bit paranoid, a little bit *touchy* when it comes to the subject of other people wanting to be the father of the revolution." I looked up at the monument, and saw the Father's sword, and the fierce expression on his face, and his fierce rearing horse, and thought that my father might be right.

"I'd probably rather be the grandfather of the revolution, anyway," I said, picturing my grandfathers, kind, leathery men who read the newspaper in the morning and who, for the rest of the day, played card games—Rook, Tile Rummy, Pitch— that no one else had played for fifty years. They seemed happy, is what I'm saying, the kind of men who you wouldn't mind being when you grew up.

But my father shook his head gravely and said, "I bet the father of revolution killed the grandfather of the revolution so that he could be the father of the revolution in the first place. I bet the grandfather of the revolution is an even more dangerous thing to want to be than the father of the revolution."

When my father said this, I thought of how my mother sometimes called him Eeyore when they were fighting, and sometimes even when they weren't. It wasn't at all unusual to hear, in the middle of one of their whispered kitchen arguments, my mother saying loudly, "Why do you have to be such an Eeyore all the time?" and my father saying, "Because you make me that way," and my mother saying in a high braying voice, "Eeyore! Eeyore!"

"OK," I said, ready to give up on the subject and go get our drinks. "Whatever." But my father took a step closer to me and put his gloved hand on my arm and gave me a begging look that said, "Please, please don't stop."

And so I looked around the Square to see what else I might want to be when I grew up. As I said, it was snowing, and windy, too, snow devils swirling around our feet and the base of the monument, and so there weren't too many people walking around the square. But there were the usual vendors standing behind their tables with the folding legs: the white couple in matching dashikis selling their canned preserves and jars of pickled vegetables, the man trying to get you to sign his petition in favor of light rail, the man with the watch cap and the long white beard who was peddling what his handmade sign said was handmade rope. There were coils and coils of the rope on the table in front of him.

"I guess I could be the Hangman of the Revolution," I told my father.

He seemed to consider this for a minute, and as he considered it I considered him. As I said, his hair was gray, but he still had most of it and it hung down over in his forehead and over one eye in a way that suggested youth, even if it was just the memory of youth. He had lines coming out of the corners of his eyes and mouth, but they hadn't yet begun to drag his face downward. They didn't make him look old, yet, but they didn't exactly make him look happy, either. "I just don't know how to make you happy anymore," my mother would say during their fights. And maybe that's why I always liked meeting him at the Square every Friday at four and having a drink afterward: because it always seemed to make him happy.

"I just don't see it," my father finally said, and then went to explain why it wasn't really plausible for me to be the Hangman of the Revolution: because the hangman no longer hanged people, hanging people was by now probably considered an embarrassing relic of an earlier wave of the revolution. No, nowadays the hangman would probably use an enormous hypodermic needle to inject Enemies of the Revolution with some lethal poison. "And you know how you are with needles," my father said. He was right: I was not so good with needles, I did not like needles one bit, I tended to make involuntary little retching noises when the *subject* of needles was even raised. "Not that I blame you," my father said. He then admitted that, for my sake and for the sake of my inoculation records, he'd always acted like getting stuck in the arm with a needle was no big deal for him, and that there was no reason for me to act like it was a big deal, either. But really, he now said, he didn't much care for needles himself, didn't like way the metal shaft, or blade, or whatever you called the needle when you weren't calling it a needle, gleamed in the overhead light; didn't like the way the nurse or doctor had to *flick* the needle before using it; didn't like the way a drop of the fluid hung there, quivering, from the tip of the needle until it fell onto the latex gloved hand of the nurse, or in this case, the hangman of the revolution, who no longer was allowed to hang people, and who I definitely would never grow up to be. "Can you imagine being executed like that?" my father asked. His voice and eyes were faraway, and I could see him still seeing that needle. "It would feel way too clinical and also way too graphic," my father said, "like you were being executed by the dentist who was also the pornographer." A man and a woman in fleece vests were walking by with their cups of to-go coffee just then, and when they heard my father say, "executed by the dentist who was also the pornographer" they stopped blowing on their cups and looked at us weirdly before moving on. "Can you imagine executing someone like that?" my father asked.

"I guess not," I said.

"So, being the Hangman is out," my father said.

"When's Mom meeting us?" I asked.

"I don't think she is, bud," my father said, although I already knew this without him telling me. My mother hadn't met us for dinner on a Friday night for a long time, so long that it'd begun to seem like maybe she'd never met us, that it was something I'd only imagined. Just that morning, in fact, before leaving for school, I'd asked my mother if she was meeting us for dinner on the Square later that night, and she smiled sadly and ruffled my hair and said, "I don't think so, honey. Besides, I think your father has something he wants to talk to you about."

And I suppose I knew what my father wanted to talk to me about, too. Because the night before all this, during the last of my parents' kitchen fights, I'd heard my father say, "I just don't think I can just stick around and see you be with someone else." He whispered this, but it was loud enough for me to hear, and it was also loud enough for me to hear my mother whisper back, "Where are you going to go?" and then my father whisper back, "I'll let you and Charlie know when I get there," and then my mother whisper back, "So that's it, then," and then my father shouted back, "But I worry about what's going to happen to Charlie! I worry about him so much!" and then my mother said back, flatly, "If you were so damn worried about him, then you wouldn't...." My mother didn't finish the sentence but she didn't need to: I knew what she thought my father wouldn't do if he were so worried about me, and I know my father knew, too, because he said to her in a strangled voice, "I know," and then the next day, after he'd told me I couldn't be the Hangman of the Revolution, he asked, "What else of the revolution do you think you might want to be?"

Why are we still talking *about this?* is what I wanted to say. *Why don't you just tell me you're leaving already?* But then I noticed something about my father's eyes: normally they looked wet, like either he was about to cry or had just stopped crying; but now they were dry, and bright, like he had this really great idea and wanted me to have it, too. And after thinking for a few seconds, I thought I knew what the idea was: as long as he, and I, didn't know what of the revolution I was going to be, as long as he didn't know what was going to *happen* to me, he wouldn't be able to stop worrying about me. And if my father wasn't able stop worrying about me, he wouldn't be able to leave me, either.

"What about the Voice of the Revolution?" I said.

My father nodded, then held his chin, like he was considering this or pretending to consider this. "No," he finally said, "you're way too quiet." Then, he made a circular motion with his right index finger to tell me to keep going. I did, and in this way, the possibility of my being the Poet of the Revolution, the Strong Arm of the Revolution, the Conscience of the Revolution was raised and then dismissed. Each time he decided I was ill suited to be this or that of the revolution, my father seemed to get more and more hopeful, and I did, too. By the end, I was looking wildly and happily around the Square for ideas. "What about the Horseman of the Revolution?" I said, looking at the monument, and then was sorry I did, because my father's eyes seemed to get wet and the corners of his mouth dropped. I knew what he was thinking: about how, when I was eight, I'd ridden a horse at the county fair and the guy leading the horse around and around the paddock by a rope said, "Hey, you're pretty good at this. You could do this for a living." *I'd be a terrible horseman of the revolution*, I wanted to tell my father. And then: *Please don't leave*. But then he looked away from the horse, and at the man behind the card table asking people to sign the petition in favor of light rail, and my father's eyes got bright again. "Except there are no more Horsemen of the Revolution," he said, cocking his head in the direction of the guy and his petition. "No Ironhorsemen, either. The Carmaker of the Revolution has seen to that."

After that, neither of us said anything for a while. I just stood there, watching the monument and the snow and thinking of how easy it would be to go on this like forever: to meet my father in the Square every Friday and reaffirm that he still had to worry about me, that he still had to stay, no matter what was going on with my mother, no matter who she was with, no matter how much pain it would cause him. Our talks about all the things of the revolution I could not be would be part of normal life—that's what I was thinking, and that must have been what my father was thinking, too, because he asked finally asked me a normal question: "How was school today?" he wanted to know.

"Not so good," I admitted.

"Why not?"

"Don Treadway called me a retard," I told him.

"A retard," my father said—not like he was outraged, but like he was thinking about it, and then I was, too. I was thinking of what it would be like to be the Retard of the Revolution. I could see myself, after all the years and waves of the Revolution and still, my face would stay unlined, my hair still brown and full, my smile still empty and innocent. Every Wednesday, I would go to the pool—to the YMCA pool in the winter and the outdoor public pool in the summer--and stand ankle deep in the shallow water in my garish flowered trunks and watch the babies splash around with their mothers, watching and watching the babies for so long, and with such an obvious expression of longing on my face, that it would make the mothers uncomfortable and about to get out of the pool and go complain to someone when, I, the Retard of the Revolution, would wade over to them and ask if I could hold their babies. "No, I don't think that's such a good idea," the mothers would say. And that would not bother me. I would just shrug and wade away, seemingly as unaffected by this rejection as I had been by all triumphs and terrors of the revolution that had happened up until then, all the triumphs and terrors yet to come. I could do all that. I could be that person, and my father couldn't, and that was why I could stay, and that was why he had to leave.

"Oh don't cry, bud," my father said and he hugged me and I let him.

"I'm not," I said, because I was trying not to.

"It's OK," my father said. "You're going to be OK."

"I know I am," I said. My father let go of me. He looked at me for one long last time, then kissed my forehead, and told me he loved me. Then, he turned and walked away, and I never saw him again.

Murderinging The Dead Father

(with apologies to Donald Barthelme)

Terese Svoboda

Dead, but still with us, still with us, but dead. There is nothing unusual about the foot except that it is seven meters high. All working night and day for the good of all.

My children, the Dead Father said. Mine. Mine. Mine.

Smug, isn't he? said Julie.

A bit smug, said Thomas.

A bit, the Dead Father said.

Thomas flang his sword into a bush.

He is dead only in a sense, Thomas said.

I am offended, said the Dead Father.

Children, he said. Without children, I would not be the Father. I never wanted it, it was thrust upon me. I had to devour them, hundreds, thousands, feefifofum, sometimes their shoes too, get a good mouthful of childleg and you find, between your teeth, the poisoned sneaker. I suppose I could have hired someone to peel them for me first.

He does go on, said Julie.

The projector is set up for the projection of the pornographic film. The Dead Father is not allowed to view film, because of his age. Outrage of the Dead Father. Damn your eyes, etc.

Dragged him all this distance without any rooty-toot-toot. Is that a threat?

Oh yes I read about it. In the Svenska Dagbladet.

They came then to a man tending bar in an open field. Shocking, said the Dead Father happily. Never in all my years—

The stomach heaved like a trampoline in the direction of its admirers.

Quite wonderful, said the Dead Father. I was offended, of course.

Suffer, Julie said.

A son may after honest endeavor produce what some people might call, technically, children. But he remains a son. In the fullest sense.

Oh, I am tired of you, Julie cried. Tuff titty.

Unfuckingbelievable, said Emma.

Yes, the Dead Father said, and on that bank of the river there stands to this day a Savings & Loan Association. A thing I fathered. That was when I was young and full of that zest which has leaked out of me and which we are journeying to recover.

No tale ever happened the way we tell it, said Thomas, but the moral is always correct.

You want to try on my belt buckle? The Dead Father unbuckled his belt and handed it to Thomas.

I took it. Away from you.

A marvelous speech, said Julie. Would you autograph my program?

Beautifully done, said Thomas. Are you free for lunch?

They found the Dead Father standing in a wood, slaying. A toad escaped. His smoking whinyard wiped upon the green grass. Temporary happiness of the Dead Father. I do inspire awe, said the Dead Father.

If I pop one will you pop one? If I pull this little white string, will you explode?

Okay Fat Daddy, she said, show me how to dance.

It is obvious but for a twist of fate I would be his and not yours, said Julie.

Oh, yes, Thomas said, he has something. I would not dream of denying it.

But remember there was a time when he was slicing people's ears off with a wood chisel. Two inch blade.

Expectoration of bhang juice. (emphatic).

How do you get him around the bends in the road?

He is articulated.

What if he were just a little more dead?

Does he really want to hear the answer? asked Thomas. No, I don't think so.

The Dead Father plodding along, at the end of his cable. Thomas opened the box and found a knife. Use it, said the Dead Father. Cut something. Cut something off.

You must've studied anatomy.

In extenso.

We feel it's a scotomizing, you might say. A darkening of the truth.

What is wrong with me, the Dead Father shouted. You are making me feel like the Congress of Vienna. The Dead Father fell down on the ground and began chewing the dirt of the road.

Why is that man, that one of you, the distinguished looking one, being dragged?

He is a father, said Thomas.

Terrible news, said the man, you can't bring him in here. That thing there would scare the children out of their wigs, did they but get a glimpse of it.

Happiness of the Dead Father.

Mad fathers stalk up and down the boulevards, shouting. If he cries aloud, "*The cat's in the cassock and flitter-to-thee morseso stomp it!*" remember that he has already asked you once to "stomp it" and that this must refer to something you are doing. So stomp it.

Two leaping fathers together in a room can cause accidents. The best idea is to chain heavy-duty truck tires to them, one in front, one in back, so that their leaps become pathetic small hops. The best way to approach a father is from behind. Thus if he chooses to hurl his javelin at you, he will probably miss. Text-fathers are usually bound in blue.

I'm goin' to whack you, kid, if you don't stop cryin'. You got three minutes.

Of all fathers, the fanged father is the least desirable. There are twenty-two kinds of fathers, of which only nineteen are important. Give thanks. These penises are magical, but not most of the time. Yes, let her touch it (lightly, of course) but briefly. The matter is as I have presented it.

Yet the children, one by one, disappeared. Good.

It is not necessary to slay your father, time will slay him, that is a virtual certainty. You must become part of your father, but a paler, weaker form of him.

Pop one of these, makes you feel better.

It's her own gutter she's after.

The letter a failure but I mailed it nevertheless.

You must've studied English.

The Dead Father flung himself to the ground. But I should have everything! Me! I've always been very careful with my passport.

Thank you, said Thomas. See? It's bent. Thomas handed him the pornographic comic book. It will keep you occupied.

I don't want to be occupied.

Count your blessings.

I don't want to make a will, said the Dead Father. Dash my wig! I'm too young.

He turned a page.

My sword is gone, said the Dead Father, but I have a spare sword, back at the city. Do you want Regina?

I only wish to have everything tidy.

Older people don't really like younger people, the Dead Father said. The Dead Father gave Thomas his keys.

Oh, he said, I see.

Great wreaths of every kind of flower standing about on stands.

You're not alive, said Thomas. Remember?

That's all? said the Dead Father. That's the end?

Did I do it well? asked the Dead Father.

The Penis

Jeff Parker

I.

ON THE TWENTY-FIFTH DAY OF MARCH, an unusually strange incident occurred in St. Petersburg, Florida. The esthetician Daria Bezugla, who lives across from the world's largest gift shop on 18th Ave. N. and whose last name in Russian means "without corners," woke up early and sensed the smell of bread. Raising herself a little in bed, she saw that her wife, quite a respectable lady, who very much liked her cup of coffee, was taking a just-baked loaf of bread from the Zojirushi bread maker.

"Today, Jenny Jackson, I will not have coffee," said Daria Bezugla, "but instead I'd like to have some hot bread with onion."

Let the fool eat bread; so much the better for me, the wife thought to herself, there'll be an extra portion of coffee left. And she threw the loaf of bread on the table.

Daria Bezugla settled at the table, poured out some salt, prepared two onions, took a knife in her hands, and, assuming a significant air, began cutting the bread. Having cut the loaf in two, she looked into the middle and, to her surprise, saw something. Daria Bezugla poked cautiously with her knife and felt with her finger. "Firm!" she said to herself. "What could it be?"

She stuck in her fingers and pulled out—a penis!...Daria Bezugla began rubbing her eyes and turning it around: a penis, precisely a penis! and, what's more, it seemed like a familiar one. Terror showed on Daria Bezugla's face. But this terror was nothing compared to the indignation that came over her wife.

"Where did you pull that penis off, you beast?" she shouted wrathfully. "Floozy. Drunkard! I'll denounce you to the police myself. What a bandit! I've heard from three men already that you pull penises so hard when you give Brazilian waxes that they barely stay attached."

But Daria Bezugla was more dead than alive. She recognized this penis as belonging to none other than assistant treasurer Smith, whom she waxed on or about the thirtieth of every month.

Unlike most of Daria Bezugla's regulars, both men and women (though more and more it was men these days) who asked for the same basic Brazilian every time they came in, assistant treasurer Smith of the Republican Party of Florida liked to mix it up. One month it'd be the Bermuda Triangle, another the Martini Glass, then the Champagne Glass, the Eye of the Tiger followed by the V For Vendetta, and so on. It was not uncommon for her clients to get erections during the procedure and frankly speaking nothing could have impressed Daria Bezugla less. Nonetheless she utilized them when they appeared. At first she did this out of pity for her embarrassed clients, taking it so naturally and functionally normalized the situation. But she soon realized the practical advantage to having a lever to help with what she thought of as counterpull, something to yank the skin with while ripping the wax strip. Regarding the age-old question as to whether or not bigger was better, Daria Bezugla had no opinion and not even a passing interest. She could say with certainty however that bigger was definitely better for counterpull, and the opposite held true. The opposite was the case with assistant treasurer Smith. His penis reminded her of a button. Daria Bezugla could hardly find purchase on it. To make matters worse, assistant treasurer Smith always said, "Your hands are eternally cold, Daria Bezugla"—and Daria Bezugla, a great cynic, would always reply with a question: "And why should they be cold?" Why should they be cold indeed? Wasn't she handling hot wax with those same hands? "I don't know, sister, but they are cold," assistant treasurer Smith would reply.

There was no doubt it was assistant treasurer Smith's. More than anything else, it resembled a button. It had the two beauty marks, which, he'd once told her, he christened Lewis and Clark.

"Devil knows how it happened," she said finally, scratching herself behind the ear. "Whether I came home drunk yesterday or not, I can't say for sure. But by all tokens this incident should be infeasible: for bread is a baking matter, and a penis is something else entirely. I can't figure it out!..."

Daria Bezugla fell silent. The thought of the police finding the penis at her place and accusing her drove her to complete distraction. She could already picture herself in handcuffs and an orange jumpsuit...and she trembled all over. Finally she took her black ninja slippers, shorts, and tanktop and, to the accompaniment of Jenny Jackson's weighty admonitions—"What could I expect from a woman named Without Corners? Without Corners, my god!"—wrapped the penis in a rag and went out.

She wanted to just pitch it anywhere, but she kept running into people that she knew leaving the Panera or cleaning up at the Monticello Inn or smoking behind the Outback Steakhouse, someone who would begin at once by asking, "Where are you off to?" or "Who are you going to see so early?"—so that Daria Bezugla could never seize the moment. At one point, she had already dropped it, when the booming voice of a bike cop said, "Excuse me, miss, you've dropped something there, right there!" pointing at the penis in the rag and Daria Bezugla had to pick it up and put it in her pocket. Despair came over her, particularly as more and more visitors to the World's Largest Gift Shop and the Sunken Gardens filled the sidewalk.

She decided to go to Crescent Lake: might she not somehow throw it in?...But I am slightly remiss for having said so little about Daria Bezugla, a worthy woman in many respects. Daria Bezugla, like every decent Russian-American artisan, was a terrible drunkard. And though she waxed other people's pubes every day, her own was full bush. She wore the typical uniform of a woman of her station. A tank top, cut-off jean shorts and the black ninja slippers which seemed appropriate only for ninjas and those working in salons of one type or another.

This worthy citizen was already on the bridge over Crescent Lake. First she glanced around and then leaned over the rail, as if looking under the bridge to see if there were lots of turtles floating there, and quietly threw down the rag with the penis. She felt as if a three-hundred-pound weight had suddenly fallen from her; Daria Bezugla even grinned. Instead of going to wax the pubes of functionaries, she was heading for an institution under a sign that read "Bud Light" when suddenly she saw at the end of the bridge the bike cop.

She went dead; and meanwhile the cop beckoned to her with his finger and said, "Come here, my good woman. Tell me what you were doing standing on the bridge."

"By God, sir, I'm on my way to administer a Brazilian wax and just stopped to see if the Marabou stork was here, standing among the thistle." Daria Bezugla was fascinated with the universally acknowledged world's ugliest bird, the marabou stork, which had probably escaped from a zoo or something and waded about in Crescent Lake some mornings. Its head reminded Daria Bezugla of so many scrotums—she felt a nearly overwhelming desire to wax it.

"Lies, lies! You won't get off with that. I saw you drop that item again." It was still floating near one of the turtles. "Be so good as to answer!"

"I'm ready to offer you Brazilian waxes, on the house, every four to six weeks just as we advise, to let the hair grow back to a length that makes it easier, that is to say, makes the whole process more comfortable, for you and, frankly, for me, officer, with no objections."

"No, friend, that's trifles. I have three estheticians to Brazilian wax me, and they consider it a great honor. Kindly tell me what you were doing there."

Daria Bezugla blanched.... But here the incident becomes totally shrouded in mist, and of what happened further decidedly nothing is known.

II.

The assistant treasurer Smith woke up quite early and went "brr...." with his lips—something he always did on waking up, though he himself was unable to explain why. He went to the bathroom to pee, and, still half asleep, he reached for his penis, to direct the stream into the toilet; but, to his great amazement, he saw that instead of a penis he had a perfectly smooth place. Frightened, he began feeling around with his hand to find out if he might still be asleep, but it seemed he was not. The assistant treasurer Smith jumped out of bed, shook himself: no penis! He dressed himself, found that while his pants fit more comfortably, they bunched a bit in that area, and he flew straight to the chief of police.

But meanwhile it is necessary to say something about Smith, so that the reader may see what sort of assistant treasurer of the Republican Party of Florida he was. Some assistant treasurers have learned degrees, they work their way up, starting out on the grassroots front line of the party, hawking conservative positions to the receptive denizens of Pinellas County, one of the largest Republican districts of the largely Republican state of Florida. These hardworking assistant treasurers pay their dues and work diligently for the sake of a cause that they believe in. Other assistant treasurers buy their way in with cash and celebrity. Assistant treasurer Smith was of the latter type. He had made a small fortune off several of the sleaziest Tampa strip clubs and then cultivated a public persona with a short-lived but wildly popular radio show. He had held the rank of assistant treasurer for only two years, and therefore could not forget it for a moment; and to give himself more nobility and weight, he never referred to himself as assistant treasurer, but always as Trezh.

Smith had the daily habit of strolling Central Avenue. The collar of his shirt front was always extremely clean and starched. Smith sought a post suited to his rank—State Senator, Lieutenant Governor, Governor, Ambassador, Secretary of Health or Education or Head of the EPA, A True Senator…the assistant treasurer spot, a functionary one to be sure, was meant as a springboard and a springboard only. Smith would not have minded getting married, but only on the chance that the bride happened to come with substantial capital. And therefore the reader may now judge for herself what the state of this assistant treasurer was when he saw, instead of a quite acceptable if undersized penis, a most stupid, flat, and smooth place.

As bad luck goes, there was not a single Uber nearby, and he had to go on foot. He walked with an awkward stride, feeling a distinct lack in the crotch department, a lack so profound it felt as if passersby could see it on his face, as if something was missing there. He popped into a McDonald's and went to the bathroom to inspect the matter again. *But maybe I just imagined it that way: it's impossible for a penis to vanish so idiotically,* he thought. But indeed it was gone. "Devil knows, what rubbish!" he said, spitting. "There might at least be something instead of a penis, but there's nothing...."

Biting his lips in vexation, he walked out of the McDonald's. Suddenly he stopped; before his eyes an inexplicable phenomenon occurred: a limousine pulled up in front of the marina; the door opened; a gentleman in an impeccable suit jumped out, hunching over, and ran into the marina, across the dock, and into a monumental yacht. What was Smith's horror as well as amazement when he recognized him as his own penis! At this extraordinary spectacle everything seemed to turn upside down in his eyes; he felt barely able to stand; but, trembling all over as if in a fever, he decided that, whatever the cost, he would await his return to the limousine. Two minutes later the penis indeed came out. He was wearing a Dolce & Gabbana Jacquard Two-Piece Tuxedo Suit. By all indications he was going somewhere on an official visit. He hopped into the limousine and it pulled away.

Smith nearly lost his mind. He did not know what to make of such a strange incident. How was it possible, indeed, that the penis which just yesterday had been attached to his groin, unable to walk or wear accouterments of any kind with the occasional exception of a cheap condom—should be in a four-thousand-dollar suit. He ran after the limousine which luckily had not gone far and stopped in front of the downtown church.

He hastened inside, making his way past a row of old beggar women with bandaged faces and two openings for eyes, at whom he had laughed so much before, into the church. There were not many people at the mid-day service, but Smith saw him kneeling on a pew. The penis had his face completely hidden under the lapels of the suit jacket and seemed to be praying with an expression of the greatest piety.

How shall I approach him? thought Smith. *By all tokens, by his Dolce & Gabbana suit, one can see he's a fat cat, a donor no doubt. Devil knows how to go about it!*

He began to cough beside him; but the penis would not abandon his pious attitude for a minute and kept bowing down.

"My dear sir," said Smith, inwardly forcing himself to take heart, "my dear sir...."

"What can I do for you?" the penis said, turning.

"I find it strange, my dear sir...it seems to me...you should know your place. And suddenly I find you, and where?—in a church? You must agree...."

"Excuse me, I don't understand what you're talking about. Explain, please."

How shall I explain it to him? thought Smith, and, gathering his courage, he began:

"Of course, I...anyhow, I'm an assistant treasurer. For me to go around without a penis is improper, you must agree. Some homeless dude hanging out near the banyan trees can sit without a penis; but, having prospects in view...being acquainted, moreover, with ladies in many houses: Marlene Bruddox, the wife of a vice-chairman, and others...Judge for yourself...I don't know, my dear sir...." (Here assistant treasurer Smith shrugged his shoulders.) "Pardon me, but... if one looks at it in conformity with the rules of duty and honor...you yourself can understand...."

"I understand decidedly nothing," replied the penis. "Explain more satisfactorily."

"My dear sir...." Smith said with dignity, "I don't know how to understand your words... The whole thing seems perfectly obvious.... Or do you want to... But you're my own penis!"

The penis looked at the assistant treasurer and scowled slightly.

"You are mistaken, my dear sir. I am by myself. Besides, there can be no close relationship between us. Judging by this Men's Warehouse suit of yours, it's highly unlikely that we run in similar circles...."

Having said this, the penis turned away and continued praying.

This threw Smith into despair. He walked away and paused for a moment under the fake, cardboard colonnade to collect himself. When he turned the penis was nowhere in sight.

"Ah devil take it," said Smith. He called an Uber. "Hey cabby, drive straight to the chief of police!"

"Is the chief of police in?" he cried, entering the front hall.

"No he's not," the officer at the desk said. "He just left."

"Worse luck!"

"Yes," the doorman added, "not so long ago, but he left. If you'd come one little minute sooner, you might have caught him."

Smith found the Uber he'd just gotten out of still sitting in front of the police station. He hopped in. "Drive. I'll pay you double your fee, whatever you say."

"Where to?" said the guy.

"Straight ahead!"

"How, straight ahead? There's a turn here—right or left?"

This question stopped Smith and made him think again. He realized that the knave and cheat, his penis, had already behaved so shamelessly at their first encounter, he might split town if word got out the police were looking for him. What he needed was to go straight to the people, a description of his qualities so that anyone meeting him could bring him to him or at least inform him of his whereabouts. Personally, he didn't have enough followers, but the social media accounts of the Republican Party of Florida had millions, many in the immediate area. He only needed to talk to that little twerp, the social media clerk who posted all their announcements. He told the guy to drive to the Republican Party Headquarters, and all the way there he never stopped hitting him on the back with his fist, saying: "Faster, you scoundrel! Faster, you cheat!" "Chill out, dude," the guy said, shaking his head and stepping on the accelerator. When they finally pulled up, Smith, breathless, ran into a small reception room, where a goateed clerk in a skinny tie and spectacles sat at a desk, holding a pen in his teeth and looking over a spreadsheet on a massive display that, it seemed to Smith, must be a plasma TV and not a computer display at all.

"Winston!" cried Smith. "I need to get something out on the party social media."

"Excuse me," said the goateed clerk, raising his eyes for a moment and lowering them again to the spreadsheet. "I beg you to wait a bit."

Smith felt that he could lose it on the little clerk, but if he lost it Winston would never agree to send his message out and where else could he get instantaneous exposure like that. No, he would cool out and after it was all over and he had his penis back in his pants where it should be, he would whisper into the ears of the chairman about Winston's late nights and public interludes at the Flamingo Resort which wouldn't at all sit well with the party's Christian donors.

"Of course, my dear sir," Smith said and sat in one of the brown leather chairs with gold buttons. Instinctively he adjusted his crotch and was reminded by the absence that there was nothing to adjust.

The clerk puzzled at the spreadsheet. His face was mere inches from the giant screen. Each cell on the spreadsheet before him was large enough to contain one of his eyeballs. He moved his head as he took in other cells, occasionally tapping at the keyboard without looking at his hands.

"What can I do for you?" he said at last, turning to Smith.

"I ask..." said Smith, "some swindling or knavery has occurred—I haven't been able to find out. I only ask you to advertise that, whoever brings this scoundrel to me will get a sufficient reward."

"I see. Well, it's somewhat unusual. But you are the assistant treasurer. Let me see if I've got this straight, the runaway was your pet?"

"My pet? Pet? That would be no great swindle. The one that ran away was...my penis...."

"Hm! What a strange name! And did this Mr. Penez steal a large sum of money from you?"

"Penis, I said…you've got it wrong! My penis, my own penis, disappeared on me, I don't know where. The devil's decided to make fun of me."

"Disappeared in what fashion? I'm afraid I don't quite understand."

"I really can't say in what fashion; but the main thing is that he's now driving around town done up like one of our top donors. And therefore I ask you to announce that whoever catches him should immediately bring him to me asap. Put yourself in my shoes, how indeed can I do without such a part of the body, a man of my position and a man of my talents? On Thursdays, I call on the wife of the party treasurer himself—and she has a very pretty daughter—they are my very good acquaintances, and consider for yourself, now, how can I…I can't go to them now."

The clerk fell to pondering, as was indicated by his tightly compressed lips.

"No, I can't run such an announcement on the party social media," he said finally, after a long silence.

"What? Why not?"

"Because. The party may lose its reputation. If everybody starts writing that his penis has run away, then…People say we publish a lot of absurdities and false rumors as it is."

"But what's absurd about this matter? It seems to me that it's nothing of the sort."

"No, I absolutely cannot place such an announcement."

"But my penis really has vanished."

"If so, it's a medical matter. They say there are people who can attach any penis you like. I observe, however, that you must be a man of merry disposition and fond of joking in company."

"I swear to you as God is holy! Very well, if it's come to that, I'll show you."

"Why trouble yourself!" the clerk went on. "However, if it's no trouble," he added with a movement of curiosity, "it might be desirable to have a look."

The assistant treasurer unbuckled his pants and lowered his underwear with both thumbs.

"Extremely strange indeed!" said the clerk. He tipped his head back slightly as if to see if anything was hidden underneath. "The place is perfectly smooth, like a just-made pancake. Yes, of an unbelievable flatness!"

"Well, are you going to argue now? You can see for yourself that you've got to post it. I'll be especially grateful to you."

"It's not fitting for Facebook, or even Twitter. I'm looking out for you. You'll be eaten alive. You should give it to someone with a skillful pen, who can describe it as a rare work of nature and publish the little article in *Science* or *National Geographic*" (here he glanced back at his spreadsheet), "for the benefit of the young" (here he wiped his nose), "or just for general curiosity."

The assistant treasurer was totally discouraged. He left the party headquarters in deep vexation and went to see the police commissioner, a great lover of sugar. Smith entered just as he stretched, grunted, and said, "Ah, now for a nice two-hour nap!" And therefore it could be foreseen that the assistant treasurers arrival was quite untimely; and I do not know whether he would have been received all that cordially even if he had brought him several pounds of candy. The commissioner received Smith rather drily and said that after dinner was no time for carrying out investigations, that a respectable man would not have his penis torn off, and that there were assistant treasurers of all sorts of organizations whose underclothes were not even in decent condition, and who dragged themselves around to all sorts of improper places.

It must be noted that Smith was an extremely touchy man. He could forgive anything said about himself, but he could never pardon a reference to his station. He shook his head and said with dignity, spreading his arms slightly, "I confess, after such offensive remarks on your part, I have nothing to add...." and left.

He returned home scarcely feeling his legs under him. It was already dark. Dismal or extremely vile his apartment seemed to him after this whole unsuccessful search. Going into his bedroom, the assistant treasurer, weary and woeful, threw himself into an armchair and finally after several sighs, said: "My God! My God! Why this misfortune? If I lacked an arm or a leg, it would still be better; if I lacked a nose, it would be bad, but still more bearable; but lacking a penis, a man is devil knows what: not a bird, not a citizen—just chuck him out the window! And if it had been cut off in war or a duel, or if I'd caused it myself—but it vanished for no reason, vanished for nothing, nothing at all...."

Assistant Treasurer Smith, having put all the circumstances together, supposed it would hardly be unlikely if the blame were placed on none other than Mrs. Bruddox, the vice-chairman's wife, who wished him to marry her daughter. He himself enjoyed dallying with her, but kept avoiding a final settlement. And when the mother announced to him directly that she wished to give him the girl's hand, he quietly eased off with his compliments, saying that he was still young and had to serve some five years more, until he turned exactly forty-two. And therefore the vice-chairman's wife, probably in revenge, decided to put a spell on him, and to that end hired some sorceress, because it was by no means possible to suppose that the penis had been cut off; no one had come into his room; and the esthetician Daria Bezugla had waxed him on Wednesday, and the penis had been there for the whole of Thursday and Friday—he remembered that and knew it very well; besides, he would have felt the pain, and the wound undoubtedly could not have healed so quickly and become smooth as a pancake.

Just then there was a knock at the door and in came a fit police officer wearing a short-sleeve uniform suggestive of bike cop, the very same bike cop who, at the beginning of this tale, was standing on the bridge at Crescent Lake.

"Excuse me, sir, did you perchance lose your penis?"

"Right."

"It has now been found."

"What's that you say?" cried assistant treasurer Smith. Joy robbed him of speech. He stared with both eyes at the policeman standing before him. "How did it happen?"

"By a strange chance: he was intercepted getting onto a ferry to the Keys. And he had a passport long since filled out in the name of some official. The strange thing was that I myself first took him for a gentleman. But fortunately I was wearing my spectacles, and I saw at once that he was a penis. For I'm nearsighted, and if you're standing right in front of me, I'll see only that you have a face, but won't notice any nose or beard. My mother-in-law—that is, my wife's mother—can't see anything either."

Smith was beside himself.

"Where is it? Where? I'll run there at once."

"Don't trouble yourself. Knowing you had need of him, I brought him with me. And it's strange that the chief participant in this affair is that crook of an esthetician from 18th Ave. North, over by the world's largest gift shop, who is now sitting in the police station. I've long suspected her of being a drunkard and a thief, and only two days ago she swindled a latte out of Panera without paying. Your penis is exactly as it was."

Here the policeman went to his pocket and took out a penis wrapped in a piece of paper.

"That's it!" cried Smith. "That's it all right. Kindly take a cup of tea with me today."

"I'd consider it a great pleasure, but I really can't: I must go to the food stamp office...Everything's gotten so expensive... I've got my in-laws living with me, and the children—the oldest in particular: he's whip smart, but there's nothing for his education...."

Smith understood and, snatching a Benjamin from his wallet, put it into the hand of the officer, who bowed and scraped his way out.

On the policeman's departure, he carefully took the found penis in his two cupped hands and studied it.

"That's it, that's it all right," assistant treasurer Smith kept repeating. "Yes, there are both Lewis and Clark," he said, referring to his beauty marks.

He almost laughed for joy.

But nothing in this world lasts long, and therefore joy, in the minute that follows the first, is less lively; in the third minute it becomes still weaker, and finally it merges imperceptibly with one's usual state of mind, as a ring in the water, born of a stone's fall, finally merges with the smooth surface. Smith began to reflect and realized that the matter was not ended yet: the penis had been found, but it still had to be attached.

"And what if it doesn't stick?"

At this question, presented to himself, the assistant treasurer blanched.

With a feeling of inexplicable fear, he rushed to the table. His hands were trembling. Carefully and cautiously he applied it to its former place. Oh, horror! The penis did not stick!... He held it to his mouth, warmed it a little with his breath, and again brought it to the smooth space; but in no way would the penis hold on.

"Well, so, stay there, you fool," he said to it. But the penis was as if made of wood and kept falling to the table with a strange, cork-like sound. The major's face twisted convulsively. "Can it be that it won't grow back on?" he repeated in fear. But no matter how many times he put it in its proper place, his efforts remained unsuccessful.

Smith resolved to write to the vice-chairman's wife the next day, before filing a complaint, on the chance that she might agree to return to him what she owed without a fight. The content of the email was as follows:

Dear Madam Bruddox,

I am unable to understand this strange act on your part. Rest assured that in behaving in this fashion you gain nothing and will by no means prevail upon me to marry your daughter. Believe me, I am perfectly well informed concerning the story of my penis, as well as the fact that none other than the two of you are the main participants in it. Its sudden detachment from its place, its flight, its disguising itself first as an official and now finally as its own self, are nothing else but the results of witchcraft, performed either by you or by those who exercise similarly noble occupations. I, for my part, consider it my duty to warn you: if the above-mentioned penis of mine is not back in place this same day, I shall be forced to resort to the shelter and protection of the law.

Nevertheless, with the utmost respect for you, I have the honor of being

Your humble servant,

Paul Smith

III.

Perfect nonsense goes on in the world. Sometimes there is no plausibility at all: suddenly, as if nothing was wrong, that same penis which had worn a Dolce & Gabbana tuxedo suit was back in its place—that is, precisely between the thighs of assistant treasurer Smith. This happened on the 7th of April. Waking up and instinctively going for his morning pee, he saw: his penis! He grabbed it—yes, the penis! "Aha," said Smith, and in his joy he nearly Macarenaed all around the room.

There was no way to explain it. Mrs. Bruddox replied in a fashion that suggested she had had nothing whatsoever to do with it and that she was still hoping that he would take her daughter's hand. It was better, assistant treasurer Smith decided, not to question good fate.

While appreciating the repatriation of his penis, Smith noticed that his pubes had come in quite a bit so he went to Daria Bezugla's salon. She greeted him as timorously as a cat that has just been beaten for stealing lard.

"Tell me first, are your hands warm?" Smith cried.

"Yes."

"Lies!"

"By god, they're warm, sir."

"Today, I would like to have the Martini Glass."

Smith got undressed and assumed the position. Daria Bezugla slathered the hot wax strips all around his crotch. Then, as happened when she dug into some of the tighter spots, he grew an erection, if you could call the small lever that popped up there an erection.

Look at that! Daria Bezugla said to herself, glancing at the penis. Normally she would take it directly, perfunctorily, making it less awkward for everyone that way. But on the count of recent events she was not herself. She dithered. At last, lightly, as cautiously as one can imagine, she raised two fingers so as to grasp only the tip of it.

"Oh-oh watch out," cried Smith.

Daria Bezugla dropped her arms, more confused and taken aback than she had ever been before. Finally, she fished for the edges of the wax strips and though it was quite difficult and inconvenient for her to rip the wax without any counterpull, she finally managed to wax a complete martini glass into his pubes.

Afterward Smith went out into the town, veritably prancing. Everywhere he went, he sat and crossed his legs and made a big show of adjusting himself. And the penis also sat where it belonged, below the martini glass, as if nothing was wrong, not even showing a sign that it had ever gone anywhere. Freshly waxed, he felt himself anew. And after that assistant treasurer Smith was seen eternally in a good humor, smiling, and chasing after decidedly all the pretty ladies.

Such was the story that occurred in St. Petersburg, Florida, the limp, runaway penis dangling off the Southeastern corner of our country. Only now, on overall reflection, we can see that there is much of the implausible in it. To say nothing of the supernatural detachment of the penis and its appearance in various places in a Dolce & Gabbana tuxedo suit. And then, too—how did the penis end up in the baked bread and did Daria Bezugla herself...? No, that I just do not understand, I decidedly do not understand! But what is strangest of all is how authors choose subjects (and subsequent authors take up those subjects, changing things here and there so that what is symbolic in one is literal in another or what is literal in one is symbolic in another and so on and so forth)...I confess, that is utterly inconceivable, it is simply...no, no, I utterly fail to understand.

And yet, once you reflect on it, there really is something to all this. Say what you like, but such incidents do happen in the world—rarely, but they do happen.

Peredelkino

Jane Ridgeway

THE GLOSSY BLACK RAVEN with smoked windows glided to a stop at the curb, spinning up muddy droplets from the gutter. Mishka beside me took a quick, neat step away, but I, too slow, stood with the water running into my shined shoes as the new commissar, Dzimov, emerged from the car, unfurling toward the dull dark sky. His coat buttons strained across his thick animal chest, as if he were moments away from ripping his uniform to pieces and dropping to the ground like a wild boar, running off into the savage woods.

The last commissar had been a mean little gnome of a man, but soft-hearted in his own way. He loved beautiful things: planted hundreds of fruit trees in front of the commissar's mansion and sent matching saplings to Stalin. There was a poem by M— that he liked so much he learned it by heart, and would recite it, smiling into a cup of wine, even after the poet's arrest.

He was the one who had promoted me, bringing me back from my posting abroad. No one was sure yet what he had been taken away for—espionage, or homosexuality, or something of that sort—but he and his deputy were gone after a good run of two years, which was longer than they usually lasted.

The old commissar had been a bureaucrat at heart, who liked to enrich his own coffers and collect imported cigars.

The new one, per the local gossip, was a true enthusiast.

Mishka and I hurried behind Dzimov as he walked briskly toward the offices, his fingers running over the Raven's flank as he passed, caressing the car like a sweating, exhausted horse. Since Dzimov's arrival, this car had already become known on the streets of Moscow, where he liked to make his driver cruise in slow circles in the afternoons when school let out, and where mothers grabbed their daughters' elbows to get them quickly off the streets.

In the dim corridor inside, we passed shabby relatives queued up with lunches and letters for the prisoners, waiting listlessly in front of the reception office that would not open for several hours. Later, the informants with their anonymous letters would wait alongside them.

Dzimov's deputy produced an order for us on a single sheet of paper, to go to the home of a particular writer and to bring him in, in connection with his international associations, and to gather evidence from the home before it could be destroyed by his accomplices.

"Go to the wife first," Dzimov said, "she'll know where the scoundrel is, even if he thinks she doesn't." This author had been well known in the previous decade for his presence at fashionable, and sometimes scandalous, parties everywhere from Moscow to Paris.

Dzimov asked if we knew the way to a particular block of apartments. When I said yes, he fixed his eyes on me for the first time and laughed.

"You? Our foreigner? I don't think your colleague will thank you if you do the navigating! Listen to that accent!"

I told him that I had been born and raised in the city, before leaving for an education in Europe, and my posting abroad.

"Thought you'd come back now, did you, and bring a little culture to us simpler souls, is that it? An act of charity, I see!" Dzimov pushed the warrant into Mishka's hands. "You watch out for your sophisticated friend, here!" he said.

Mishka handed the document to me as Dzimov strode down the hallway away from us, shedding his coat and shaking it off in irritation when it stuck on his thick arms.

"Too bad about the accent," Mishka said as we walked back to our own offices to meet the driver who would take us to the apartments. "Nothing you can do about it now. This isn't a good time for the old boss's favorites. You should have made a statement against him. But there'll be someone else— that's the ticket for you. Next time someone from the old gang gets pushed out, you put a nasty note in their file. That's how you win him over. You've just got to let him know you're one of us, Squints."

When I first returned to the Moscow office, the other men had called me Specs. Though I had gotten used to leaving my eyeglasses at home, the nickname had only been replaced, and now every day passed somewhat out of focus.

In the main office, one of the new captains who had come in with Dzimov, a robust young man with golden hair, was standing over my desk, throwing letters in the waste bin.

"Such news of the world!" he said. "I feel like I've gotten a proper education just from reading this. What do you think, Squints, do I look like a scholar now?" he asked with a smile before laughing and walking away.

The young captain was always neatly dressed and clean-shaven, his belt buckles shining and shirt creased sharply. He gave off an aroma of tobacco and health, cologne and good fortune. I had grown up among many boys like him; for fun, they would dip a piece of paper in kerosene and tie it to a cat's tail, then light it and watch it run yowling down the street. At the same age, I had disappointed my father deeply when he took me out to the woods to learn to shoot. When a beautiful buck had come into sight, snorting audibly in the cold morning air, I had fired my rifle wildly at a scrap of bright red cloth snagged in a tree. He told me, after that, that I could not be trusted with a gun again.

Mishka watched as I gathered the envelopes, edges split open and ragged as wounds, from the trash. All were from my family still overseas. I smoothed them and tucked them in the inner pocket of my coat.

Our driver was waiting for us, drinking a cup of tea. Though I knew we did not have time to stop for a cup ourselves, as the hot steam rose from his tea, it seemed to me like the warmth rising from the baths my mother would draw for me after school, back home. Both thirst and memories reached down inside my chest and closed hands around my breastbone, yanking hard.

We took one of the good cars, not an old van, to go to the apartment, as a sign of respect for this writer, who after all was an important man. I had imagined, once, many years before, what it would be like to encounter him at one of his fashionable parties, and to make intelligent conversation, perhaps to see him nod with approval and stroke his chin.

In the apartment building, many doors were boarded up already, as if the plague had passed there. As we took the elevator up to the floor of the writer's apartment, I imagined the inhabitants of each floor listening, ears pressed to the wall, listening to the elevator's mechanical whir, waiting to hear that we had passed them by.

"Do you know what I did when Tanya left me?" Mishka asked me. He told me that he used to go to her apartment at three in the morning, just like this, and bang on her door, *bam bam bam*, the way we do when we're coming to arrest somebody. He would hear her footsteps creeping toward the door until her tremulous voice called out his name. "She was always hoping it was only me," he said, with a dreaming cast to his eyes.

The author's wife opened the door the barest sliver, looking frightened but already prepared, wearing her shoes beneath her dressing gown. The author himself was not there, she said. So we took her with us to his dacha at Peredelkino.

In the early morning dark only the sketched outlines of the cottages were apparent as we moved into the countryside, the paved road giving way to spring mud beneath the tires. The author's wife clutched her hands and swayed without comment as the car bounced over pot holes. Cabbages and pumpkins hummocked the ground in garden plots narrow graves. Ghostly, white-bearded goats moved among wild lupins.

The author's dacha was modest, trimmed in white, set back behind a tangle of heavy, fruit-bowed tree limbs.

When we stepped from the car I heard a curious cooing and looked all around for the source, which transpired to be a dovecote perched above the cottage door. Pigeons peered from the little holes in the dovecote, watching us and commenting on our arrival, as gossipy as the neighbors who would peer through the spyholes in their doors when we walked down an apartment building's hallway.

Mishka had the wife knock first and call out, so the author would open the door. And so he did. He was a weak-chinned little man with spectacles on his nose, behind which were wakeful, intelligent eyes.

"You've brought guests," he said to his wife after a pause. "But I have nothing to feed them!"

The little author smiled thinly, eyes flitting nervously over Mishka and landing on me.

"Do I know you?" he asked. "Have we met?"

I was momentarily silent with surprise, but felt Mishka's gaze on me and so said, "Here now, show us inside!"

The writer looked down at the doorstep strewn with downy pigeon feathers. "All right," he said, "all right, that's fine."

"You don't suppose we're going to stand here all night, do you?" I said, pounding a fist against the lintel. The pigeons above us fluttered with alarm.

Mishka took charge of the author and his wife, while I searched the cottage's office. The author's space was austere, meticulous. There was a locked trunk which, forced upon, was full of letters from around the world. A stack of thick, expensive-feeling writing paper, all cut to the same precise size, sat neatly on the desk. I was glancing over half-written pages, dawdling to read a sentence here and there, when I heard a cry from the other room, and hurried to gather all the papers together.

The author's wife was pressed up against the wall, a hand over her mouth and her other arm outstretched. Mishka was standing over the author, who was crawling on all fours like a stunned animal struck once in the slaughterhouse but not finished off.

I watched his hands sweeping the floor, following their arc until I saw the glimmer of his spectacles on the boards just in front of my feet. I looked from the author to his wife, to Mishka, and stepped forward heavily. The glass lenses crunched beneath my boot, wires deforming and twisting. The author's hands ceased sweeping the floor at the sound of the eyeglasses cracking to pieces. He was still for a moment, taking a deep breath, and then looked up at me with my arms full of papers.

"I haven't finished those," he said. "Please, my friend. You don't need those."

I gave him a kick, which he scurried away from. "Get up, you sly fox."

Mishka smiled at me like a proud father as he escorted the author and his wife from the house, while I struggled to carry all the papers.

Outside, the morning sun was beginning to shine over the horizon at a severe angle, blinding us with the intensity of a bare bulb. The author squinted into the light, and I saw that one of his eyes was beginning to swell, a single red moon that would soon blacken.

The pigeons watched us, murmuring to each other, as we loaded the author and his wife into the car.

The author's wife was silent on the way back to the city. The little man himself turned to me and said, "I guess you don't get much sleep, do you?" Startled, I laughed before I could stop myself. The sun was rising, now, lighting up the dew on the fields as we drove, making the whole world look slick and glossy, as if one could slip right off of it and fall away to some other place.

Arriving at the prison, the author kissed his wife once, then strode through the gates unassisted. His wife watched him go, then turned to me, dazed.

"Will they give him a cup of hot tea?" she asked. "He can't start the day without one."

Dzimov was so pleased by our arrest, and by the chest full of letters implicating the author's correspondents, that Mishka and I merited an invitation to a dinner at his home.

The old commissar's prized orchard was overgrown, vine-strangled. When I entered the dining room, Mishka was already recounting the famous author's capture.

"He put up quite a fight, didn't he?" Mishka said merrily, slinging an arm around my shoulders. In front of this audience of other officers, every embellishment was surely meant as a favor to me.

I agreed with each part of Mishka's story, nodding and smiling along as he described how the writer, groveling, had begged for mercy and then tried to make a break for it. Mishka explained in gruesome detail how I had stomped one of the man's pigeons to death. It almost seemed true, the way he told it, and all the more so as I warmed from drink and conversation.

Dzimov finished the evening with a party trick, ordering his cook to stand against the wall with an egg balanced on his head. The man seemed to be working hard not to shake. When Dzimov cracked the egg into smithereens with one shot, leaving the cook with yolk dripping down his forehead and into his eyes, I applauded furiously.

When I arrived home late that night, I took my letters out from my coat pocket and looked them over. I had noticed before when my mail seemed to have been steamed open and shut back up, but never before had it simply been torn open.

One letter was from my nephew, who was a university student in Austria. I could no longer remember what precisely I had last written to him, but he seemed to be continuing a conversation about whether to remain in art school or abandon it for a more practical trade.

"In these difficult times," my nephew wrote, "the only thing I'm certain of is that art can save us."

I put on my spectacles to write back to him, eyes sore and watering from the long day spent half-blind.

That night I fell asleep more easily than most, sure that the next time, after Mishka's heroic tale, my mail would not be thrown in the trash. I dreamed: and in my dream, Dzimov's party bustled merrily around me, the other officers smiling at me where I stood with my back to the wall, a pigeon atop my head. The animal cooed, its talons scratching my scalp as Dzimov sighted his revolver. I shut my eyes before the shot, and did not know if it was egg or viscera, the pigeon's blood or my own, that dripped down my face and ran into my eyes, making them burn.

POSSIBLY FORTY SHIPS

TIBOR FISCHER

"YOU KNOW HOW THIS WORKS."

"May I assure you that not only do you not have to torture me, you don't even have to bother threatening me with torture."

"And may I assure you that I have no shame or hesitation in torturing a defenseless old man. So, talk."

"How can I assist your curiosity?"

"You know. The war. The Trojan war. I'd like to hear the understory, the truth."

"The truth? How do you define—"

"Let's not start that. I've heard the Stories and I've heard some stories. I've heard the...talk...I want the what-I-saw from someone who was there."

"I was there."

"You know what I'm asking. Everyone swears this was the greatest of the wars, everyone has heard the stories of the glories. Everyone says the heroes' names will be lip-ferried to the future. Tell me about the War at Troy."

"How do you define war? What is a—?"

"Chop two."

"You still have some fingers left and a good chance of not bleeding to death."

"Thank you. I didn't like those fingers anyway. And a man my age needs so few."

"Let's start again. No word-fiddling."

"The stories are...well, what everyone says about the war... they don't have much to do with what happened. The stories and the lived, they're as similar as, say, a horse and a leech."

"The beginning?"

"Of course. Now if I were to point out every untruth, we'd be exhausted—"

"I'm in no rush."

"First of all, probably, in all likelihood, the most important thing to say about the Trojan War is: there was no war."

"No war?"

"Well, and please let me finish, because I honestly want to satisfy your curiosity, it again depends what you intend when you confer the title of war. If you see war as a few ships sinking in the middle of the waves, a few dozen warriors in armor, frankly not as gleaming as it could be, being welcomed whole-heartedly by the water, far, far away from Troy, if you see that as war, then it was a war."

"Helen?"

"Helen's not a story. She was the wife of Menelaus. Good-looking, not that good-looking, but good-looking."

"Paris?"

"Real."

"And he abducted her to Troy?"

"Not in the widely accepted use of the word abducted. Menelaus forced her on Paris. He was bored with Helen; once you've had your wife in fifty-six positions, it's not the same, is it? Menelaus wanted Troy's wealth and an excuse. He told Paris he was divorcing Helen and he would consider her removal a courtesy. Paris was only up to position number five or so, so he cheerily agreed. And Paris returned to Troy with a barkful of wine, congratulating himself that Greek and Trojan relations were as happy as a mouse in a granary."

"And Menelaus got together an army of all the Greeks?"

"A few of the Greeks. Have you ever asked anyone for a favor?"

"They all said they were there."

"Afterwards, they all said they were there. Have you ever noticed how when something important or funny happens everyone pretends they were there? I was there when Kalchas ate a whole pig in one night. There were five of us there. Since then I must have met fifty people who insist they saw Kalchas eat a whole ox. Stories recruit. Give people what they want and you'll never go hungry."

"So Agamemnon and Menelaus set sail for Troy?"

"No, not King Agamemnon. He sent floral encouragement."

"So the Greek fleet set sail for Troy?"

"Again, it depends how you care to define fleet, but we set sail for Troy."

"And the fleet sank?"

"All but one ship."

"How?"

"There are at least two ways of looking at this. Some would argue that Menelaus and his intimates were guilty of serial impiety and that the Gods meted out punishment by storm."

"Or?"

"Menelaus was poor. As kings go, a beggar. The reason he wanted to loot Troy was not greed, but need."

"Ornamentation is all. Only those who are poor at greed speak ill of it. What is the point of being in a world full of appearance, if you don't have the appearance you want? How will your greatness be known, if it can't be seen from afar?"

"Your greatness is unmistakably great—"

"My greatness doesn't require your notice. Back to Troy."

"Menelaus owed a lot of money to Xanthos the Wine-trader. You owe a man one goat, it's your problem; you owe a man fifty good-yielding goats, it's his. Xanthos had concluded that the only way he would get any money back was by investing in war. So Menelaus's battle-fleet was really Xanthos's salesmen."

"*Not much in the way of preparation?*"

"'*Is this a good idea, going to fight Troy?*' *That thought was slinking around. But no one knew how well defended Troy was. One or two traders had been there. 'So what's Troy like?' 'They've got walls.' Okay. 'Have they got towers?' 'How do you define tower? Yeah, they've got towers.' So they have walls and towers. Does that help you much? 'Are they moderately assailable walls or not?' 'How do you define moderately assailable? I'm not sure, it was a long time ago. Maybe.'*"

"*And why did you go?*"

"I had nothing better to do. My brother had the goats, and I was a bean-grower whose beans shunned life."

"*This Xanthos was to blame?*"

"No. Unless you count good sense as a crime. Out at sea, the weather turns nasty. You didn't have to be a bore of windlore to see this was bad. Xanthos orders us to land. Menelaus who has been afloat twice, on a lake, says no, we can ride it out. Xanthos's crew, these old salts, they're so maritime, they're practically fish. They're terrified, some of them are crying like little girls, growing the sea. Menelaus's bodyguard, his favorite killers, they're terrified. They're doing everything to look like brutish bronze-drivers, but fears are bulging out of them like horns.

"You understand how when someone's really helped you, you really hate them? Menelaus hated Xanthos, because he owed him everything, and because he made money from wines of no fame. 'People don't want good wine, they want bad wine, cheaply,' Xanthos used to say. 'Bad wine is, even if you piss into it—which I do—wine. You only go out of business worrying about quality.' Menelaus countermanded Xanthos not because he thought he was right, but because he had to. The storm comes, and afterwards we're the only ship in sight, in a corpse and wreckage soup.

"No one said anything. There was much toe-gazing. Even for a king, it's embarrassing losing your entire army before the war starts, although army might be an over-generous epithet for the band of simpletons, thieves, fishermen, ne'er-do-wells and a pet seal under Menelaus's command. There was even one group who thought they were travelling to Egypt. They had paid a hefty fare.

"Finally, Menelaus breaks his silence. He has Xanthos weighted and thrown overboard. 'That's the debts. Now, a slow story-building trip home,' he proclaims. 'It was Xanthos's impiety and recklessness that cost us everything. Any questions?' No questions. We're glad to be alive and heading home, all of us vowing never to leave land again. Then the lookout shouts that there are three ships approaching, with Trojan insignia.

"We're almost crippled, we can't outrun them and the storm must have pushed us into Trojan waters. 'Listen carefully,' says Menelaus. 'There was no army. There was no war. We love those Trojans to profanity.' I'll say this for Menelaus: he would have decapitated his mother for a bowl of fresh figs and he couldn't organize a cockfight, but he could lie from dawn to dawn.

"The Trojans board. They're no fools. Word has reached them about Menelaus. They see the floaters, but since Menelaus hails them like brothers, as brothers you actually like, they take him to Troy, which he maintains is exactly where he wants to go.

At Troy, we are greeted like dead rats in your water supply. The idea of slitting Menelaus's throat and using him as fertilizer is visibly given consideration. Maybe they admire the way he lies, but King Priam and the others listen.

Menelaus stands there and declares he came to Troy because he wanted a Trojan wife now that Paris has a Greek one. He adores their culture so much he wants to learn how to speak Trojan, to recite some of their great epics and to gorge on that famous Trojan fried pigeon. They listen to him, pondering fertilizer.

"But he's their jug. And everyone has a sister or daughter they want to get rid of. They think about fertilizer and selling the rest of us into slavery, but maybe it's better to have a marriage of some sort. And if they kill Menelaus maybe, possibly, someone in Greece will seek revenge, or perhaps the deities of hospitality will be vexed. They marry Menelaus off to a very minor princess so ugly she has to sneak up on a fig tree to pick the fruit. They tattoo Menelaus with Trojan emblems, since he professed such admiration for Trojan culture, including one on his back, which, I was reliably informed, signified 'I am Priam's jug.' And they make him recite thirty lines of poetry every evening."

"That's it?"

"Nothing happens for a long time. Menelaus doesn't want to go home. He realizes he's a contender for jug of jugs. And, curiously, life at the Trojan court, even as a jug, isn't bad. He has all he wants, and the fried pigeon is, as they say, remarkably good. He becomes a very fat, very drunk fat drunk. The Trojans mock him mercilessly. They can't believe he's still draining their hospitality years after arriving. 'You're sure you're not the Menelaus who said he was going to burn Troy?' 'Lose any armies today, lard lord?' Priam joked that some rulers have pet lions, some have pet giraffes, I have a pet king. The court magicians used to work him into their displays."

"And what were you doing?"

"I was retinue. Troy had its own bean-growers, so I had to tag on to the ankle of Menelaus. The great Belly-Grower said to me, 'You. I don't know how long we'll be here or how I'm getting out of this, but we need some verses to cover our red, smacked arses. You, you'll be the wordwarden. We need a yarn when we get back. Get me some good stories and well-wrought epithets or I'll have you impaled. Meanwhile, I'll have a think about how to get out of this.' He thought about it for six years."

"So Troy's towers were untouched?"

"I didn't say that."

"But you said there was no war?"

"You don't need a war to raze a city. It was six years after we had arrived. I was reconciled to dying there. I could have got back, but I, like Menelaus, had nothing to go back to. I got a bit of fried pigeon every now and then, so crisp and yet so succulent, and I had done some work I was very proud of, creating Beta, a bare-breasted princess warrioress of Greece who has a six-year single-combat with Zeta, the bare-crotched princess warrioress of Troy, at very close quarters, if you follow me. Who doesn't like to hear about over-oiled women locking limbs? Well, Menelaus didn't. He felt it wasn't martial enough. Beta's sidekick was a wise-talking tortoise, but Menelaus didn't like the tortoise either. He had been bitten by one as a child.

"One day, Menelaus is staggering around the dock, more grape than man, as a Greek ship is putting out to sea. Some kid, eleven or twelve, on the deck spots Menelaus and makes this well-known gesture of contempt."

"That one."

"Menelaus goes mad. He's been snooked by the Trojan nobility every day for six years, but he has accepted this as a ruse in his master plan of revenge. This Greek kid is too much. He dives in and almost drowns trying to reach the ship, he wants to throttle the kid so badly.

"He summons his retinue. There are five of us left. Helen, of all people, helps us; her conjunctions with Paris aren't as regular as they had been. And Menelaus has an advantage in his plotting. He's a well-established buffoon no one in Troy takes seriously. He announces he's going home, but he wants to leave a present."

"*This wouldn't be the Trojan Horse?*"

"How did you guess? Yes, Menelaus wants to leave an offering. Helen did the real work, she was very clever. It wasn't easy doing things unnoticed there, but as I said they'd stopped worrying about Menelaus. They had other, slimmer, more vigorous enemies, who were sniffing around in the distance with their chariots, prodding. We built the giant horse, as the stories relate."

"*But no warriors?*"

"No one remotely heroic. Menelaus still had two bodyguards, but one had a bad back and the other was blind."

"*No Achilles then?*"

"Ever meet anyone who knew Achilles?"

"Yes."

"Then you can take pleasure in knowing they were shameless liars. Achilles was...my private joke. A skinny child who liked wearing dresses. I scattered some truth in the stories. Any ten-year-old girl with spirit could have bested him. They only took him on the expedition because with so many men on a lengthy military campaign, they might need a jug.

"He reached Troy with us where he made clothes for the women. He was the only one of us exiles to be successful there."

"And God-like Odysseus?"

"Odysseus was god-like. Powerful, good-looking, cunning, daring. The man all men would want to be. Of course, he never got to Troy."

"What happened to him?"

"This I didn't witness. This is tittle-tattle, though my sources are trustworthy. Odysseus was with us in the storm, then...no sign. What I heard was, after several misfortunes, he eventually adorned the King of Ethiopia's bed, pumped full of poppy and bummed into madness. He was there for some fifteen years. At the end they said you could drop a vole into his rear."

"So he didn't want to get back to Ithaca?"

"Have you been to Ithaca? I'm not surprised he wasn't in a rush to return to kingship, to listen to someone complaining about their goat's yield being affected by their neighbor's incantations or someone filching some beans. The King of Ethiopia got tired of him or died. So he, the poppy-eater, had to go home. It's not surprising that none of his companions made it back from the Ethiopian court with reminiscences to offer around the fire during the long winter evenings. Nor is it a wonder he butchered everyone he found in his palace."

"And how did the real Trojan Horse work?"

"We built it with fire-growing materials, it was stuffed not with soldiers but with hay, as a horse should be. We waited till the high point of the summer, when it was dry and hot, and we placed it next to the houses of the poor. A four-legged bonfire, ready for its flame.

"Menelaus wasn't in the mood to be hacked to death by irate Trojans, so his plan was to sneak away at night, to be already well out to sea, cherishing the distance and the darkness, while his army stayed behind and took the risk of igniting the Horse. The army was me and the bodyguard with the aching back."

"Your loyalty was remarkable."

"It depends how you define loyalty. The two of us were ordered, at the least wakeful moment of the night, to light the horse and as many buildings as we could. Then to rush to a boat through wrathful Trojans and row out to find Menelaus, waiting for us gratefully, in the middle of the dark. Not a proposition that guaranteed a tranquil old age.

"If I had refused, being the former lackey of an unpopular fat drunk in a foreign city who had tried to destroy it, that wasn't a very appealing proposition. On the other hand, carrying out the orders was suicide. At the last minute, as we stood in front of the Horse with our torches, the bodyguard with the bad back cursed his luck for not going blind and decided to go to the Trojans to squeal about Menelaus's treachery.

"It was strange. I was getting what I wanted when I had followed Menelaus: to burn down Troy. There I was, clutching a torch, with the opportunity to ash an entire city single-handedly with a single hand. I was getting what I wanted but in a way I didn't want. In a cowardly, despicable way, that would almost certainly bring me death. And even more exasperatingly, it wasn't just a cowardly way to attack your enemy, your hosts who'd given you some fried pigeon, not as much as you'd like...but it would be a cowardly, anonymous way.

"No one would ever know it was me, because Menelaus would seize any glory, and so even that small clique who admire perfidious arson and shameful murder, even that small clique wouldn't admire me."

"So you chose to burn Troy? I'm looking at the man who destroyed Troy?"

"No, I did what most people do when faced with a difficult choice. I did nothing. I stood there with the torch, wondering. As my mind circled like a dog chasing its tail, the wind chased a spark into the Horse and that was that. I was knocked off my feet by the blast. I ran and I ran with an interest in running I'd never had before.

"I got to the boat and rowed out into the darkness. I didn't think I'd find Menelaus, but I figured it would be safest to be out at sea, that I might be picked up by someone who wouldn't kill me straight away. When I hit Menelaus's ship, I don't know who was more surprised, him or me. I could see the weighting-and-throwing-overboard order being given consideration. 'Why aren't you dead?' he observed, doubtless thinking it would be inauspicious to kill a man with such luck."

"Your fortune does seem to be good."

"Men with good fortune usually have ten fingers and a plate of fried pigeon, Trojan style. Miles out, we could see the flames feasting on the city. We could see, whatever might remain, Troy was broken. Helen and Menelaus stood together like the old couple they were and watched a city burn, tired. It is a pity pleasure can't, like a stream, flow endlessly out of one person. There would be fewer burning cities.

"Bearing in mind I'd won his war for him, Menelaus could have said thank you in a brief, insincere, offensive monarch-like way, when no one was listening.

"I only have one real regret. I have my disappointments and I wonder how my life might have been if I hadn't embarked for Troy or if Menelaus the Fat-Gatherer hadn't been so stupid or if I had taken one of the trade routes out of Troy to see what was there; but that's the unknown, you don't know whether there's a friendly bosom or a rusty dagger lurking. I wish I'd been braver or cleverer, but my only regret is that I didn't tell Menelaus, more pig than man, to his face what I thought."

"But then you wouldn't be here. What I don't understand, if what you say is true, is why didn't Menelaus make you, as the wordman, give him unlimited praise? Why does he take such little glory in the stories?"

"The fat hadn't softened Menelaus's mind. He wanted the story to grow, to hide the truth, so he told me to make him a spectator. He knew if the story was his slaughtering everyone, no one would swallow it, but this way he could be a small part, but a part of a glorious story. He knew he couldn't be greedy here, he had to give away the spoils imaginatively. Agamemnon and Odysseus and the many others who weren't there wouldn't refuse the glory of city-sacking, and no one could be too jealous of a hero like Achilles, who didn't exist and who was dead to boot. It's one thing to lose, another to see your hated rival win.

"They say a great God once came in disguise to a goatherd who gave him hospitality. In return, the God offered the goatherd any wish. 'Ah,' said the goatherd, 'there is a man in the village who has a black goat. This goat is the envy of all, its milk flows day and night and is beyond compare. It makes the best cheese in the region. He is becoming rich from this one goat.' What do you think the goatherd asked for?"

"Ten goats like the black one?"

"No."

"Of course not. A thousand goats."

"No. The goatherd asks for the black goat to sicken and die."

"I grew up with the stories, old word man, and found no point to war because we were in infant battles, the crumbs fallen off the heroes' table for us ants. I sobbed because I couldn't have been at Achilles' side. My ambition was poisoning me, but now I can see the throne is vacant. Have you ever seen a real hero?"

"How would you define a hero? I would say someone who is cheerful when there is no reason to be cheerful invites admiration."

"I wouldn't. Now to more important matters. Now your mouth can change history."

"Tell a story that is wanted and it will stick to ears like tar. Tales of bravery are so popular, because that's as close to bravery as most of us will ever get. But, what is praised everywhere but welcome nowhere?"

"The truth?"

SHAME THE DEVIL

PAUL ELWORK

LET'S SAY I'M A REPORTER working for a small paper in a small town, and I'm covering the campaign of a local businessman-turned-politician—someone whose fame and infamy have tangled up into one thing, someone mobs of people love and truly love to hate, a legend or a disgrace depending on who you ask, a man known for battering his enemies in public speeches and for saying things others won't in front of almost anyone, a man of great wealth.

Never mind how much.

And let's call him Mr. Grace, just for fun.

Let's say my name is Larry, because I could have been Larry. Anyone could have been Larry.

So:

It's sunset in this small town—a town full of people ready to vote for him this minute, a town very friendly to his colorful ideas—and Mr. Grace is going to lead a rally of his supporters at an auditorium near town hall. He has agreed to walk the last block on Main Street with me. He has granted me an interview during our walk through the heart of town as the sun disappears in a gory puddle of shadows in the west.

As I wait at the corner for Mr. Grace's limousine to drop him off for our walk—he's almost ten minutes late by now—I can see the crowd gathered at the other end of the block. I can see the signs some of them are carrying—no doubt signs showing devotion to all the things Mr. Grace has promised to do, signs calling out the kinds of people Mr. Grace means to do these things to, in words even he doesn't feel comfortable saying in public.

Mr. Grace has only agreed to do this little sidewalk interview because I promised not to ask certain questions. My wife thinks I shouldn't have agreed to not ask those questions. She thinks I should have begged off the assignment, and that this guy has gotten enough free press by being loud and coarse and flattering the bigotry of the people in our community.

She's not wrong about that.

"But, honey," I said, "I don't need to ask him those questions. I can just let him talk—he *loves* to talk. And he'll say the things we need him to say to scare people off."

Except I also know that some of those signs are being held up by people who want to ban everything but what they think they are—people who put their trust in walls and guns over all things, except maybe a rich man who says he counts them on his side of any wall, of any gun. And I know there's almost nothing he can say that goes too far, as far as they're concerned.

Some of the crowd is still gathering, heading toward the auditorium, walking right past me in pairs and clusters—bigger groups walking down the street itself, which the police have closed to traffic in expectation of lots and lots of people. There are white-haired elderly couples, some holding hands; families with children—there's a dad with a little girl on his shoulders; groups of young to middle-aged men, noisier, rowdier, looking a lot like kids gathering for a fight in a schoolyard.

And there are the ones walking alone—almost all men—with faces set and grave, eyes on the end of the street. I don't pretend to know what's going on in their heads, but it doesn't look like joy from here.

And there are the ones who look like they've come for more than shouting and cheering—like that guy with the big swastika splashed on his upper bicep, scowling as he strides down the middle of the street.

It doesn't feel like the tension crackling in the air and making the hairs on my neck stand up has anything to do with civic mindedness at all.

And everywhere, everywhere, the American flag—on t-shirts, jackets, baseball caps, you name it.

Meanwhile, here comes the limousine. It sweeps up to the curb—shiny, black, and flawless—and out pops the man of the hour, the renowned and reviled Mr. Grace. Now, standing before me, despite his success and wealth, he looks like a weary old salesman in a suit that doesn't quite fit, still trying to sell the same shitty smile.

A couple of his guys climb out of the limo with him, and they look like some kind of cross between the Secret Service and the mob.

Mr. Grace gives me that smile, shakes my hand, and says, "Yeah, I'm late—good thing you weren't late, or we wouldn't be standing here." And in case I didn't get it: "I'd be gone and you'd have a whole lot of empty corner."

Mr. Grace's guys give a chuckle at this, without ever losing that you-watch-your-ass air about them.

The corner is anything but empty now, and the crowd begins converging all around us, now that Mr. Grace is out on the sidewalk. I wonder for a moment if I'm going to have to watch this man kiss somebody's baby.

Mr. Grace's men hold the crowd back and spread out around us. Some of the people start a welcoming chant of Mr. Grace's name, and he waves and gives them all that smile of assured triumph.

"GRACE, GRACE, GRACE"—it moves down the block, infects the people converging in the street, and crests in repeating, pounding waves in the crowd gathered around the auditorium.

Someone starts up the other now-familiar chant heard at Mr. Grace's rallies. It can also be found on t-shirts, hats, and buttons in red, white, and blue letters.

"Amer-i-ca for Amer-i-cans!"

The cheer that follows makes all the other chanting sound halfhearted. It repeats again and again, in a thunder of mingled voices. The old, the middle-aged, the young, the children—all those pale faces raised in chorus, clear in the streetlight's glow and diminishing into the shadows outside the circle of light.

And through it all, Mr. Grace waving and grinning his approval.

I've got my recorder in my hand now, and Mr. Grace leans toward it as he falls into step beside me and his men form a loose walking circle around us. Mr. Grace puts a hand on my shoulder as he leans in. "That's what we're here for—we're going to make America for real Americans again, we're going to do it right here in this great state and show the rest of the country."

"And who are the real Americans, Mr. Grace?" I shout at him above the noise.

After all, he brought it up. I agreed not to ask about some of Mr. Grace's unclear financial circumstances. I agreed not to ask about the lawsuits pending against him in his life as a businessman, the things that should be cawing after him like crows in this campaign, though no one much seems to care. But I didn't agree to not ask about his favorite thing to say since he announced his candidacy.

"You know who they are, you know who they are," he barks into my recorder. He sounds like an uncle who won't tolerate someone being a wiseass. His hand falls from my shoulder. "Everybody knows. I'm talking about real, hard-working Americans who have a right to be here and aren't going to tolerate all the nonsense anymore."

"And what nonsense is that, Mr. Grace?" I ask. My voice sounds louder to me now that his hand is gone from my shoulder, somehow. "Specifically?"

Mr. Grace looks at me sideways and gives me his real smile—which has been peeking out at rallies all along and is a matter of public record by now. That smile suggests lots of things, but I think it can be boiled down to *I win because you lose.*

"All the nonsense the politicians in the capital and the *press*" (he says this word as if it tastes bad in his mouth) "want to keep going. All the nonsense the *people* have had enough of and that I'll clean up."

At that moment, as the people he's talking about surge around us, Mr. Grace's guards let an elderly lady push through and reach out for his hand. She's short and portly, and her eyes beam out at him from under the shadow of her AMERICA FOR AMERICANS baseball cap. She's probably somebody's grandmother.

Mr. Grace comes to a full stop and takes both of her hands in his as if she's *his* grandmother, even though they can't be more than ten years apart. The lady gazes at him with her warm, almost dreamy eyes and says, "God bless you! God bless you! God bless you!" She has the sweetest smile, and she's bursting with loving kindness for Mr. Grace.

Mr. Grace thanks her, kisses the back of one of her spotted hands, and the people who have had enough of the nonsense cheer. The whole street seems to shake with it. And I can only wonder, if Mr. Grace wins, how many nice little grandmothers will cast the votes to make it so.

They won't be alone. That's the lesson of this crowd, various in most everything but skin color. And I'm shrinking from this lesson even now, as Mr. Grace turns back toward me and smirks before picking up our walk again. I'm shrinking from the questions the lesson suggests: How many more are there out there? How many more will it take?

"She doesn't have a problem understanding just what I mean," Mr. Grace says to me. "She still remembers a time—believe me—when everybody knew, when everybody knew just what I'm talking about, and we're going to bring that back—we're going to bring this state back and we're going to bring our country back."

He pours his words into my recorder, spits them at it, and the recorder gobbles them all up.

We're moving on again, making our way down the block. The police are now helping to keep the crowd from overtaking the sidewalk and surrounding us. Those people closest to us, who see us walking and talking, have fallen into the walk, too. Some of them cheer, some of them chant, but many just keep pace in great expectation and certainty that whatever else is going on tonight, Mr. Grace is here for them and with them, and their children, and their parents, and their grandparents—even with the dearly departed who couldn't be here themselves, going back generations, vast legions who would also know just what Mr. Grace is talking about.

Someone calls out, *"You tell 'em!"* Others pick up the cry, and I imagine my wife in that crowd, though she's at home, probably listening to coverage on the radio or watching it on cable TV news. I imagine her walking among them, eyes watchful on me and Mr. Grace, mouth set, closed tight.

Mr. Grace is charging ahead and I stride to keep up, as the crowd shouts for him to *tell 'em all, show 'em all, get 'em out.*

It's hard not to feel like just another fool trailing after this man who wins because others lose. It seems like we're running out of sidewalk ahead of the bigger crowd and the end of the block faster than I imagined possible, back when I agreed to only ask certain things and wanted to just let Mr. Grace talk. The realization throbs hard behind my eyes: I'm here, more than anything else, for the crowd and the cameras to see me clutching my recorder, almost tripping over myself to keep up with him.

"And all of these people here," I shout over the voices and crowd thunder, "all these working people here, what will you tell them while you're helping rich people get richer as fast as possible and leaving them behind again?"

I sound more shrill in this moment than I'd like, and Mr. Grace seems to hear all of that, too. He offers me an amused grin and looks just tickled at the question. I half expect him to burst out laughing—though I guess even he would prefer that my recorder didn't gobble *that* up.

"I don't have to explain anything to these good people," he says, his eyes bright, "because they already know—I've already told them and they know that industry and business, freed from the shackles of a crooked bureaucracy, will restore the greatness that made America loved and feared by those who should love and fear us—and *they* know who they are, the people who should love, the ones who should fear."

The chant of *Grace! Grace! Grace!* goes up again, and I'm buffeted along by Mr. Grace's men, striding hard to keep pace.

The sidewalk comes to an end ahead of us and the crowd looms, surging around the police, who get swallowed up in the tumult, and I'm ready to say, *So these people here know what they know and they know what they don't want to know?*—which I admit is starting to sound like an old Abbott and Costello routine, and not a very punchy way to get in another quick one.

At the eye of all this chaos, out of waves of sight and sound cresting on all sides, a familiar figure emerges and joins me and Mr. Grace. For me it is a figure out of time, and a moment of baffled wonder as I blink at Mr. Sumner, my high-school journalism teacher. I know the bald head, the sharp eyes behind his glasses, the rumpled coaching jacket he keeps replacing and wearing out as he passes the years keeping the cross-country team motivated and focused when he isn't wearing a tie and the striped short-sleeve button-down shirt of a bank teller. The man who told his class that the role of journalism is to tell the people what they need to know, the man who put a banner reading PROOF IS TRUTH over his blackboard, the man who said that the thing to do is to tell the truth and shame the Devil, every chance you get.

And Mr. Sumner is shaking Mr. Grace's hand, his eyes as full of warmth as the old lady's.

I stop dead on the sidewalk, goggling at the two of them, and Mr. Grace is saying, *Thank you, sir, thank you* to all the words of praise and joy Mr. Sumner is heaping on him—words I don't even catch because the AMERICA FOR AMERICANS pin on Mr. Sumner's coaching jacket is so big and colorful—until Mr. Sumner is grabbing my free hand and saying, "Larry! Look at you, making us proud!" It's the same voice he used to tell his students what happens when people quit, the same voice the cross-country coach in him poured into warnings about what happens when people can't play the long game.

I look down at my mostly limp hand in Mr. Sumner's, and as if on some signal from Mr. Grace, his Secret Service/mob guys push in between me and my old journalism teacher. Mr. Grace is putting his arm around Mr. Sumner's shoulder now, leaning in close and leading him off, with just one more smile over his shoulder for me. And the crowd opens up before them and closes up behind them as the hulking auditorium rises up above at the top of its broad, tall flight of granite steps.

The crowd pushes on all around me, and I can move forward with it or get trampled under. I can't even imagine my wife there now, in this place where she didn't belong. The crowd has consumed me and forgotten me, as if I'd never been at the center with Mr. Grace. The crowd knows what it knows and what it doesn't want to know.

The old lady, someone's grandma, knows.

Mr. Sumner knows.

The tide moves forward, and Mr. Grace ascends the stairs, arm still around my old teacher. For me, there is an almost dizzying sense of relocation—of being back here, of them up there. One of Mr. Grace's campaign staffers comes to him holding a microphone, and Mr. Grace sends Mr. Sumner on his way with a pat on the back before taking the microphone and turning to the crowd, midway up the steps. The show before the show is about to begin.

Mr. Grace raises his hand and the cheering winds down. "I just have one question for you folks," he says. "I wonder if you can help me out."

More cheering, whistling, wild applause.

"Can you all tell me who we're taking America back for, starting right here in this great state?"

They give the answer, and give it, and give it to the heavens, the voices all mingled together, ecstatic, doubtless.

All at once—and too late—it feels inevitable. All at once, the uneasiness of Mr. Grace's ascent, of his sometimes comic fear-mongering, takes on the dread and despair of watching a doomed species about to fulfill its destiny, a doomed species rising to the heights of its own invention and crashing to the depths of its own stupidity. All at once it's more than this one pro-Grace town—as if, like the generations of the dead behind this crowd, many towns for miles and miles are giving the answer under the darkening sky.

I'm stricken with it all, looking on, wishing I was back home with my wife watching it on TV.

Mr. Grace turns his finger on me. "*He* doesn't know, folks. Mr. Free Press over there."

Suddenly I'm very aware of the recorder still in my hand, thick as a brick in my fingers.

Hisses of disgust and ugly chuckles in the shadows from all sides.

"*Asshole*," more than one voice calls out, some men, some women.

Snickers from some of the children, a primal sound of playful mean that pinches the heart, just like way back when.

"*Faggot!*" a man yells from the far side of the crowd, as if he's been waiting all day to fling that word, for any reason at all.

Mr. Grace seems to not hear. "He doesn't know what we mean, he says—but oh, he knows, he knows. He just doesn't *want* to know. So maybe—I don't know—maybe he's the one who needs your help, not me. What do you say, folks? Can we help Mr. Smear Job from the *Daily Snotrag* understand what we're all talking about?"

I feel the first push from behind—experimental, almost playful. Before I can turn around or even feel the fear, I'm pushed from the side. Much harder this time, into someone who pushes me even harder the other way.

The recorder is snatched from my hand.

The crowd is chanting his name again, with a mix of devotion and rage like I've never heard before, in so many voices.

I swing my fist back at the last person who pushed. I miss and almost fall over in trying. Someone from my left lands a punch on my jaw that just about spins me, and the bright taste of blood is in my mouth.

A scared, trembling voice—that could have come from me—rises up nearby. An older woman's voice, saying, "Stop it! Stop it! We aren't animals!" It's the voice of a grandmother breaking up a tussle in the yard—only more scared than angry, shocked at what she sees. A grandmother expects stupid boys to fight in the yard. Whatever she expected to see here tonight, it wasn't this.

I catch a glimpse of her as more than one person shoves me now. Her white hair pulled back under yet another baseball cap with an American flag on it and a t-shirt that says LOVE in big, bursting letters. Her eyes are wide and staring, shivering in her face—I see all that in a glimpse. And is that a sign in her shaking hands? It is, held at her side, saying something else about love. I can't read it. She was going to hold that sign up in the auditorium and hope it meant something to someone else in that room.

Someone kicks me hard in the side and I feel something snap. I tumble into the arms of people nearby, and a shower of fists pummels down on me. Just my luck to not be standing by the lady with the love sign—I actually think this with a gut-sick and childish longing.

Before I go down, I see other people in the crowd, here and there, raise their voices against it all. I don't even hear what they say, just the outrage, the shock. It's only a few that I catch in that moment, only the ones nearby, and they sound so small all the same. I see a man, got to be in his sixties, who could be my father, pushing through the crowd toward me. He's got a love t-shirt on, too—and I'll bet others here do, as well, the small voices from people about to get punched and kicked.

Here comes the silver-haired older man in the love t-shirt. Man, I would have figured him for a Grace guy, but here he comes—teeth gritted and pushing through. He makes eye contact with me before the crowd stops him and surrounds him. And maybe, I think, maybe he doesn't look so obvious a Grace guy to me. Maybe his skin isn't so pale, but more like a shade our parents would have called *passing*—and they would have meant getting away with something, oh yes. Maybe, maybe—but it's dark out here now, even under the streetlights, and I'm going down wondering when thinking like this becomes thinking like them, these people all around me who are so sure that they know.

By now I'm down, but I can still see that look he gives me, saying, *I'm coming, I'm on my way.*

Then someone kicks me in the head and that's all I know about the screaming and the chanting and the crowd surging at the bottom of the auditorium steps, under the twilight.

Let's say the rally in the auditorium got canceled. The cops came in and broke it all up; Mr. Grace was pulled away and tucked into his shiny black car. And the people who loved him loved him more for that scene at the steps, and the people who hated him hated him more for it.

And let's say he went on to win the election. Let's say he got to be the man in that seat behind that desk. And he succeeded in doing some of the things he said he'd do, and he failed in others, and some of those things he didn't much pursue beyond shouting them at crowds, with American flags fluttering everywhere. And after Mr. Grace came and went, someone else came along, and someone else, and someone else, and the years rolled on by, and time moved on.

But let's say I never did—that Larry never moved on. Let's say Larry lived that night, more or less, for years after the bones healed (there was more than just a broken rib, by the way) and the bruises disappeared. Let's say Larry didn't hang onto the few small voices in that crowd, or the old lady with her sign about love, or the silver-haired man wading through the crowd to him, but saw a doomed species before he saw anything else, all of his days—serving what, exactly, until a gloomy dying hour?

When the Saints Come

Josip Novakovich

Davor had been wheezing for days, and he gasped in his sleep and talked about Armageddon, global warming, and the vanished Boeing 777. Even awake, he talked about 777 as the ascension airplane–all the people onboard went straight to heaven, and the rest remained on the ground, awaiting the wrath of God.

–You are not right in your head, Alana, his wife, said. Since when have you been religious?

–I used to be very pious as a kid, until I discovered girls. The way I understood it from my minister, it was either girls or God, you couldn't be a sinner and go to church, so I chose girls.

–Seriously, your breathing is terrible. You should give up smoking and go see a doctor.

–I've given up booze, that's good enough. You can't expect me to give up everything fun.

–This doesn't look like fun. Just look at you, you inhale and spit, and make faces like your tongue is burning.

–It is burning and it's not fun. I don't even get a kick from it, but I must do it. Some kind of devil, demon of smoking, has possessed me, and he's stronger than me.

−I think you have developed asthma and chronic bronchitis, just my opinion. Do your lungs hurt?

−Can they hurt? Major organs don't. It's the muscles surrounding it and bronchi and such that actually do hurt when I inhale deep.

−You have to take care of yourself!

−But why? I have lived longer than my father, who died at the age of fifty. I thought that was my deadline. I've had ten extra years. Actually I used to think I would die even earlier than that because I believed in the biblical verse, *Obey your father and mother lest your days on earth be shortened.* I was an evil kid. I fought a lot in a street gang, stole, drank, screwed around. I have no explanation why I was drawn to bad things, other than that it was some kind of freedom or that I was possessed. No matter what, I thought I would die young, maybe ten years younger than my father. That I have outlived him is obscene.

Here Davor blew out smoke, and felt like passing out. − Can you fix me some Turkish coffee?

−I will, and then we'll drive to Rebro Hospital in Zagreb.

The following day, after X-rays and blood tests, he was seated across the table from a bald pulmonologist.

−Gospodine, the doctor said. −This is the worst part of my job. He cleared his bumpy throat.

−Obviously you have bad news. Go on.

−You have lung cancer.

−Oh. Is it a death sentence?

Davor smiled hopefully. He was not surprised, but relieved. Finally, he was caught. He had not been caught stealing, cheating on taxes…but now, he was done for.

The doctor remained silent for a few seconds, scratching his bald head featuring a wine splash that looked like Sicily, and leaned forward peering into Davor's eyes.

–No, medicine has advanced. We have many ways of treating lung cancers, and almost half the people survive it. It also depends on how advanced it is and what kind of cancer it is.

–Well, you said it was lung cancer. I thought there was only one kind.

–That's what we used to think, but there are many kinds, as many as there are varieties of snow in Alaska.

–How advanced is it?

–You'll find out when we transfer you to the cancer ward for further tests.

And he found out that it was stage 3, pretty late. He was content, nearly happy – he owed it to his father to die young. He'd lived too long already. And what more could he expect of life? Yugoslavia was gone. His older son lived in Belgrade and never returned his calls, and the younger one had died of drug overdose in Stockholm, where he went as a guest worker. True, he had a fine wife, Alana, but even that had become a drag. She expected too much love-making and he found it too much work, he got out of breath fast and lost interest, his body lost interest. Now he knew why–he didn't have the lungs for it. Air literally went out of his tires.

His doctor and wife told him–he had a chance of recovery only if he quit smoking and did his best to be healthy, and he listened, although living might be more work than not living. He daydreamed about how relaxing it would be to be stone dead.

He saw his old friends and forgave everybody all the debts they owed him, demonstratively. He went to Baptist church services on Sundays and Thursdays. He would go in peace.

He enjoyed each breath he drew, each sighting of red squirrels flying from branch to branch, and he relished drinking warm spring water in the center of the park, because he knew each of these little events could be unique, and the last.

Stage III small cell cancer, survival rate fifteen percent, based on old statistics. I am done for, he thought, and strolled to his father's grave, and said, Dad, I will see you soon. Are you glad? Sunshine sifted through evergreen needles, flickered off the black marble stone, winking, and he wondered how it was possible that such a bright light came off a black stone.

At night he used an inhaler, with cortisone. And when he didn't use it, he gasped and when he was falling asleep he was not sure whether he was passing out, falling asleep, or dying. He dreamt French airplanes crashing in his backyard, snakes in his basement and in the living room, and floods coming up to the window on the second floor carrying empty coffins of his mother, father, and younger sister. And the fourth coffin was filling up with water and about to go under, and it contained a yellow figure of Davor.

In the morning, it took him a while to come to his senses. His wife brought him Turkish coffee to bed, and he drank it plain, bitter, without sugar, as Alana had read that sugar was cancerogenous. Alana studied online how to vanquish cancer with healthy foods and spirituality, written by David Servan-Schreiber, who had just recently died of brain cancer after a 15-year struggle with it. Davor ate mostly vegetables, fruits, and drank green tea. On the sly he put some sugar into green tea, which otherwise tasted like rotten hay. Hibiscus or red zinger he enjoyed plain.

–At least you are not tempted to drink slivovitza, Alana said.

–I am amazed that you managed to quit smoking with me, he said.

–After you were diagnosed, how could I smoke? I don't miss it at all.

–It might be good to get some marijuana.

–You aren't allowed to smoke anything.

–There's no proof that smoking caused my lung cancer. Maybe years of burning wood in this Dutch stove did it, maybe the war, all those bombs, who knows, maybe they had depleted Uranium, you never know. Smoking cigarettes–that could be American propaganda. Maybe I am dying from American propaganda.

Birds chirped outside the windows, swallows and finches. It was early spring in Lipik. Davor hadn't been into flowers before, yet now, he saw the world differently, and loved the forest flowers, whose names he didn't know, some white, like little bells, others blue, yellow, purple... after a dreary colorless winter, the ground had burst in the full rainbow spectrum, as though it had become heavens, and who's to say it hasn't, as our earth is part of the celestial harmony, God's design. Now that he was sure he was dying, parting from a dreary life, Davor began to feel not only tranquil, but also happy–so happy that he began to fear that he would lose these moments of beauty, that he could not hold on to them, and thus, the fear of losing the glimpses of beauty transformed itself into the fear of death, just when he thought he was completely beyond it. Certainty of death enhanced the colors of life, and the colors made Davor feel more alive than ever, and desiring to live.

And he thought, 15% survival rate. Why, I will be in the 15%. I will walk, pray, love. Maybe I will live to be 90, who is to say I won't? And 15% is an old statistic; maybe new treatments increase the chances. Maybe I'll live on carrots and walnuts, like a rodent.

But then chemo and radiation therapy came along, a dark phase of hair loss, feebleness, pain, and incessant nausea. And his wife was always there, at his side, steady, patient. Alana was his second wife. The first one left him when he was still an alcoholic as a *Gastarbeiter* in Stuttgart. Although Alana was twenty years younger than him, she stuck by him. He'd heard rumors that she'd had lovers before him, and perhaps even during their marriage, and he was jealous, but he repressed his jealousy. She certainly met a lot of people as a newsstand saleswoman. In this town and country, where half of the people were unemployed, it was a great thing to have a job. He couldn't mind that. On his own, as a car mechanic, he probably couldn't make enough for the basic bills. Twenty years ago, when the war had ended in Croatia, it was a good trade—there were many old cars which needed fixing, working on pure mechanical principles, but now, even though people couldn't afford new cars, everybody had them, somehow, and since cars were completely computerized, and Davor thought he was too old to learn new tricks, he was getting less and less work, from more and more marginal people, to work on progressively less and less worthwhile cars, for less and less. Cars that used to cost 20,000 Deutsche marks were now worth one thousand euros. Changing a clutch in a car worth ten thousand euros, he could charge 400 euros. But now that the whole car was worth only one thousand, nobody wanted to pay 40% of the car value for a peripheral part— they'd rather ditch the car up the hill outside of town for raw iron. The going rate was 100 euros for a plate-less piece of car junk. In other words, half the car value would be poured into a part, and if you added new tires, brakes, you'd spend the whole amount. To make it short, Davor, before his diagnosis with lung cancer, had become completely dependent on his wife's income. His was good enough for cigarettes, coffee, and electricity. On the other hand, he lived in the solid walls of his patrimony, a three-story red-brick house his father had built with his own hands. It was a red brick because he'd died before he could stucco it, and Davor had other priorities when he took over. It looked good in red, he claimed. So, no, he was not exploiting his wife as she had free rent in his palace, his father's palace. It was all fair. But her working in public, to come to the first point, made him jealous—sometimes she wore black stockings and exposed her chest a little too much. She did it for him, and then, when it was not him, it all was still there, for the whole town; whoever wanted to buy Jutarnji list (Moregenblatt) could take a peak at Alana's sloping breasts and shaded thighs. If he had been drinking, the way he used to in Stuttgart (oh, die Biergärten!), he would have probably come out and complained and perhaps used a heavy hand in the Balkan tradition. Sometimes he listened to Meho Puzic folk song, Majko, il me zeni il mi gitaru kupi. Oh mother, either find me a wife or a guitar, because a man must hit on something. His father had in moment of inspiration or desperation beat his mother, not often, maybe once a year, maybe less, maybe it had happened three times in his childhood, but it left him and his siblings terrified for good, and strangely, it imprinted that pattern of marriage in his mind. He was a cordial and soulful man, who, now and then, when drunk, was a heartless and soulless man, who beat the hell out of his first wife, thrice, and so she left him, to Belgrade, to marry someone there, who would continue this horrifying Balkan tradition, until she divorced him too. The younger generations supposedly didn't do it anymore but then they indulged in soccer hooliganism and war.

He took the chemo better than expected and suddenly he had more energy than he'd had in years. He had no desire for cigarettes and wondered why he had ever bothered. But that meant he couldn't go out to cafes and bars. In most of Croatia, the smoking ban in eating and drinking establishments had been lifted. The country had reverted to the Yugoslav days, becoming one huge stinging tobacco cloud. He bumped into people in the streets, and was more sociable than he'd been in decades. Memento mori improved his life tremendously, and kept him out of bars. He feared the oil and gasoline exhausts in his shop and in the streets.

If it's God's will, I will gladly go, he thought.

In the local travel agencies, he saw a sign, seven day excursion to Jerusalem, 500 euros. Four star hotel, guided tours, everything included in the price. Alana encouraged him to go. If we go, he said, there'll be that much less you'll inherit from me.

–Don't worry about that. All the money you have will be spent on your funeral expenses, she said. It's cheaper if you live than if you die.

–I've seen budget cremation advertised, basically the same price as the trip for two to the Holy Land. It's trip for one to Hell.

–No matter what, you take a trip to Holy Land, but why not try Jerusalem first. I'd like to see it too.

–But you are an atheist.

–I was raised a Catholic.

–How many times have you been to church in your life?

–I think five. Three Christmases and two Easters. Six. Once for Baptism. Missed Confirmation.

They landed in Tel Aviv on Purim and spent a night there. The city was a carnival, a Rio–people in masks, dancing, singing. The following day, in Jerusalem, Purim carried on, with people dressed in costumes, wearing masks. But the day later, cleaning crews collected the debris all over the city.

Alana and Davor didn't want to be with the tourist group, so they walked into the Old City to see the tomb of Jesus and the Western Wall on their own.

–This dry air feels fantastic, he said. Sun and dry air, a great combination.

They entered through the Damascus gate, descending the stairs past oranges and olives and nuts and sneakers and sunglasses stands. The call to prayer blasted at them from all the sides from cranky loudspeakers.

–In ancient days, they couldn't do it this loud, Davor said. They probably complain about technology and use it to complain about it . . . but what do I know?

Walking down on Via Dolorosa, Davor was dizzy from all the spices, the sun, the heat. And then they climbed on huge foot-polished cobbles behind wailing pilgrims from the Philippines. Near the entrance to the Church of the Holy Sepulchre, three soldiers in light green laughed, swaying sub-machine guns. Davor and Alana entered the gate, and faced the smooth pink-red rock, on which the body of Christ had been laid out once he had been torn off the cross. Amazing, thought Davor, knelt down at the rock, as several other people did, and kissed the rock. Thousands of people had kissed the pink marble, why wouldn't I, he thought. Well, maybe that's why–all their bacteria frolic on the rock.

–Can you imagine, Davor said. –His body was right here, on this rock.

–Yes, I'm visualizing it. Was he still bleeding?

Deeper in the cathedral, they joined a line coiling around a small ornate chapel. The cathedral contained a chapel, like a matryoshka doll, which contained the tomb of Jesus, where he resided for three days and three nights.

—Hum, so much gold, Davor said. I wonder what it was like without all the gold before.

—Yes, you kind of have to subtract the cathedral, the chapel, the precious metals, and then see the rock for what it is.

They climbed the Golgotha, just right of the entrance of the Cathedral, inside it, elevated some eight meters.

—All so close? Davor commented. —I thought they were farther apart, so you'd have to walk a little. And I thought it was a higher hill. But amazing. The crosses are here. I read that the cross of Jesus is the real cross. Empress St. Helena found it down the hill from here. Some durable wood!

—The dry air does it.

—But it's moist underground in the cave where she found it. Maybe God protected the wood so it wouldn't rot.

They went down the Golgotha, and beneath it, in stone, was the grave of Adam.

—Look, the walls are red, Alana said.

They overheard a group of German tourists. The tour guide, with a heavy Yiddish accent, said, —Das ist das Blut Jesus Christi.

—That's the blood of Jesus, you heard that? Alana said.

—Well, how could it still be here two thousand years later?

—Why not? If you believe in the resurrection, which is a bigger miracle, why not believe that this is the blood of Christ? It's the erythrocytes from the blood of Jesus, containing red iron.

—It does look impressive, Davor said.

A group of Coptic monks in brown robes sang, with beards of varying strengths and thicknesses, in the cave of

St. Helen, which being some hundred feet underground, was pleasantly cold. They chanted and danced, celebrating the cross. Davor imagined how delightful it must have been for the Empress to find the cross and to coat it all in gold and preserve it. But wasn't the church burnt down to the ground? Did the original cross burn as well? Or maybe the wood was fire-proof? Was it cedar?

Next they went to the Mount of Olives and the Gethsemane garden, and read about the temptations of Christ. Davor knelt in the church, where Christ must have knelt, and repeated his words, God, if it be thy will. . .

Alana wept as she listened to him. And said, you know what, I believe in Christ now and in God. This makes so much sense to me. And that you are suffering like that–that is already saving my soul.

The following day, they both walked to the Western Wall, passed through the security. He wore a baseball cap, and that was good enough not to have to rent a yamaka, and she rented a shawl to go to the women's side of the wall, about one third of the full length of the wall. Davor came to the wall, nearly blinded by the intense sunlight, and prayed to God. From his illness and medication, his eyes were photo-sensitive, and the white stone reflection hurt them. God, if I may address you like that here, I imagine lives don't matter to you as we all die. I beg you for a delay of ten years, only ten more years, please, and I will study your scriptures every day that I continue to live. He kissed the sun-warmed rocks. He saw notes written on paper in the cracks. Should I write one, he thought. And in what language? My English is not that good. Should I write in Croatian? Of course, God knows all the languages, but maybe German would be more convincing, being so close to Yiddish. Gott sei Dank für mein Leben.

On the way back, they walked around the walls, to Herod's gate, and not far from it, Davor saw a sign, the Garden of the Tomb. What tomb, he asked when they got close to it.

–The tomb of Jesus, the person at the door said. Would you like the map? In what language?

–Croatian.

–Yes, we have it. Here you go, God bless you.

Inside, he asked a preacher, –How is this possible? We just spent a whole day at the tomb of Jesus, and you say, this is it? I don't remember him being in two tombs.

–We believe this is the real one, the tall Englishman with yellow teeth, said. –You know the city was destroyed, so nobody really knows where the original walls were; the Ottomans outlined the city differently when they built the current walls. In the 19th century, several British archaeologists figured out that the real tomb was here.

Alana and Davor walked around the grounds, admiring their simplicity, without massive gold and silver and rubies. The tomb of Jesus had an antechamber and two parallel graves, which were at most five feet long.

–Was Jesus five feet tall? asked Davor. –Otherwise, he would have had to crouch in the grave. That would be something, a five-foot long God. Well, Beethoven was less than five feet tall.

–Look, Alana said, the stones here contain streaks of red.

–Oh, that's just iron, don't worry about it, said an English preacher. You don't need miracles to believe if you are inclined to believe.

–How can there be two tombs? Davor said. Maybe there's a third one, like a real biblical number. And what difference does it make when he was in one of them only for three days.

It's like a hotel. It's like houses in Russia, here stayed Lenin for three days.

Alana wept. —This is it, it looks so real. This is where he was dead and where he rose from the dead. It's obvious.

—What suddenly came over you? Davor asked.

A couple of big blind men held hands and prayed in tongues, under a canopy, a Russian group sang gospel on the side in squeaky voices, many out of tune, adding a note of despair. The Golgotha here indeed looked like a skull (overlooking a gas station and an Arab bus terminal with green and white buses), and that was the original meaning of the Golgotha, the Skull, and it was higher than the Golgotha in the church of the Holy Sepulchre. This one appealed to the minimalist and purist protestant esthetics, and the older Holy Sepulchre appealed to the Orthodox and Catholic Baroque tastes.

—These are just the visual aids for your faith, the English preacher, who kept shadowing the couple, said. —You can choose which one works better for you. For me, this is better, I don't have to dig through all the gold and the tourist fanfare to get to the image of the tombstone and the stone covering the tomb.

—Oh really? Davor asked. —So this is like a theater of faith?

—If you want to put it that way, yes.

Now all that was left was the Dome on the Rock, or the Holy of Holies. Orthodox Jews weren't allowed to go there, by their own religion. You should not walk into the Holy of Holies.

At the gate, a guard with a machine gun said to Alana, You aren't allowed to go in with your ankles bare. We could get you decent shoes and socks.

—Oh, no, I prefer to wait here, she said. —You go ahead, she told Davor. I'll wait for you right here.

Davor loved the sight of Mt Moriah, and marveled at the sensation of the forbidden, inaccessible, as only between 2:30 and 3:30 in the afternoon non-Muslims come in past the Arab Israeli guards.

Nobody knew exactly where the Holy of Holies was, but it was somewhere near the Dome on the Rock. Davor read in the tourist guide that King of Jordan put 85 million dollars of gold into the dome and that was when gold was twelve times less expensive than now. In other words, the dome contained one billion dollars worth of gold. But never mind that. The soil contained the blood of more than a million pilgrims and Muslims and Jews fighting for that square kilometer of arid land. He shivered at the thought, and then imagined what would happen if he stepped right into the Holy of Holies somewhere near the blue tiled golden mosque. Would he puff into nothing? Many orthodox Jews feared that, but how many of them could actually believe that? I mean, really, who could?

—Sir, are you Muslim? asked a young man at the entrance to the Dome.

—Yes, Davor said. He was surprised he so readily lied, but why would he deny himself the foundation rock, the oldest rock on earth, from which the rest of the earth was created?

—From Bosnia.

—Welcome, brother, said the man, and Davor walked in and took off his shoes and slowly walked in. While his eyes were adjusting in the dark, he smelled lots of socks, socks that had been in shoes in the hot weather for a long time, socks of pilgrims afflicted with athlete's foot, who had spent days getting here, like himself, and he nearly swooned. He turned around and put on his shoes and walked out.

How could Holy of Holies be in the fumes of overheated feet? Davor wondered. Now it made sense that Jesus would want his feet washed and oiled, though of course he didn't walk around in Adidas sneakers.

At the end of the day, he and Alana were having dinner, Dennis fish, in the garden near the hotel, and he kept looking at the limestone wall. It had the same red streaks as the stone beneath the Golgotha in the Holy Sepulchre. The streaks were common.

–Look, this is all a bunch of bullshit, he said. –There are red stains in the rocks here all over the place. It's not the blood of Jesus, and there's no foundation rock of the earth here, and it's all just a bunch of bull.

–What's come over you, why are you angry? Alana asked.

–Why wouldn't I be angry?

–You should be happy, we are in the Holy Land, I find it wonderful, I believe in God now.

–Guess what? I no longer do.

–What?

–My faith just evaporated here. It's a bunch of steam that vanished in the dry air. Nothing's left in my head, but death. Maybe I have stepped into the Holy of Holies and this is part of my death, of puffing into nothing, like cigarette smoke.

–If we hadn't come here, you'd still believe?

–Certainly.

–But you can't give up on faith now, now that you really need it.

–And that's another reason why I give up on it. I don't want to believe out of despair.

–Out of hope.

—It's the same thing. If you hope, you also despair. If you despair, you also hope. I feel nothing about the beyond. I don't fucking care.

—Watch your language, you are in the holy land.

—Oh yeah? How holy is it to herd people behind one tall wall, it's twice as tall as the wall in Berlin, you've seen it below Mt. Olive. And you saw that sign, Ich bin ein Berliner. What's holy in ghettoizing poor people? What's holy in repeating the historical mistakes? Don't do unto others as. . . well as was done unto them? This place is full of lies, even the stones lie, all three religions lie.

—Hey, quiet, calm down.

—I have no reason to be quiet. I have still some breath left and some brain, not much, so let me at least vent my belief, my lack of belief. And if I commit sacrilege, what will happen? I will die like a dog. You know what, I am already dying like a dog. And I don't want to live in a world where a bloody city like this counts as holy of holies. This is the best we can come up with, all this blood?

—Oh my God, how can you talk like that, you are frightening me.

—Sorry, I know, it's not fair. You've been so patient with me. Forgive me. But now that you have a friend in Jesus, you are all set. You'll never be lonely.

—You are right. I am so happy, and I will pray for you.

When they returned from Israel to Zagreb, they were encountered by a cold wave of weather, a slanted chilly rain, with a bit of sleet in it. Davor caught a chill and fever just from being out in the rain for a few minutes as they walked to the airport parking.

His condition worsened quickly. He no longer read the Bible or anything, as the letters shifted and swirled in his vision. He only watched soccer, although he repeated, I don't care who wins, I don't know these people, they are too rich anyway, how can I want any good to happen to a rich person. And then he'd fall asleep. Strangely enough, he woke up, and couldn't get out of bed, he could barely lift his head, but not much.

He moaned in pain. His head hurt, his bones hurt, his chest hurt.

He was taken to the hospital for an exam, and the findings were that his cancer had progressed, that it was metastasis, and now it affected his bones and his brain. He had a series of small strokes. It was hard to explain, the doctors said. His moaning became louder, and doctors administered high doses of morphine. And he didn't pray, didn't even say Oh God. He swore like a Turk, like a Croat. And then the ambulance returned him home.

Upon seeing the red bricks of his home, he laughed. –And whose blood is this in the bricks? Is it mine? Is it the blood of the Serbs killed in the Second World War here? His dog sniffed him and barked as though he'd become someone else in the meanwhile.

Now that he was bed ridden, and the doctors determined that another wave of chemo would be only detrimental at this point, that the only thing that could help would be hemp oil and morphine, his old friends and relatives began to visit. They all quieted down, unsure of whether he was still conscious, whether he was asleep or awake, and he wasn't sure whether he was asleep or awake, whether this was part of some methodical nightmare that although boring grew more and more dreadful by the hour. Nights were especially harrowing with hallucinations and wheezing.

As morning doves began to coo under his roof, announcing the thinning of the night darkness, dispersing the darkness— where did all go, where could it hide, in this universe, which is mostly darkness—he felt relief, and wondered whether his nicotine stained teeth hurt, and if they did, whether he would notice toothache among so many other shades of headache and bone-ache he suffered. He could not get out of bed, could not lift his head, and Alana tilted him to one side and another and wiped him and washed him as though he were already a corpse, or Jesus who had been taken off the cross. But no, he didn't want to think of the religious metaphor because he didn't believe, but the fact that since he ceased to believe precipitated such a swift decline tempted him to believe again. Maybe it was a divine retribution, and that it was so effective, suggested God's power at work.

His cousins came. A doctor, who worked as a cardiologist in Zagreb, and his brother, a journalist for the Croatian daily, Vecernji list, Abendblatt. He suddenly remembered how this younger one, Mirko, was four years younger, and how he'd taught Mirko, when Mirko was eleven year old, to masturbate in order to make his penis grow. —Do it every day. If you don't do it every day, it won't grow, and trust me, you do want to have a penis above average if you want to be loved by a beautiful woman. Poor shmuck, he thought, and smiled, and neither of them have any idea what I am thinking now. He opened one eye and peered at Mirko, who had grown a big beard since he'd last visited a year before, looking like Moses or Karl Marx. Or God. Not Jesus, Jesus didn't have an impressive beard, but if he was a man, even he masturbated. What were his erotic fantasies? And if he had none, was he human?

He smiled or thought he did and kind of phased out. His wife talked, and said, —His mind is going. He called from the hospital and said, I don't see anything. I was scared that he'd lost his sight, but he meant to say, I don't hear anything. The words mix up. Lucky thing he can see.

—But he can't hear?

—Usually he can't. Sometimes he has a phase when he can hear a little.

—Brain is a miraculous thing, said the doctor.

—How long do you think he has to live yet? asked Mirko. —Seven days? Nine?

—I don't know. It's not cool to predict such things, the doctor replied.

—He looks weak but somehow happy and clever.

The doctor bared Davor's shins and pressed them with his thumb, and said, —The legs are normal temperature and there's no swelling whatsoever, so it means the heart and the kidneys are doing their job despite his not moving at all. With a good heart, there's no telling how long he could last. It could be months, unless, of course, his brain suddenly shuts down the impulses through the life center.

Davor heard and understood all of this but with the excess of morphine in his body, all he could do was to grimace vaguely and good naturedly, and his wife commented, —Oh, he's so sweet sometimes, like a baby. You can see it, there's bliss in his face.

Both cousins shook his right hand, and kissed him on the cheeks and on the forehead, and left. Oh, yes, shake my masturbating hand, he thought. I will probably never do it again, and I'll never have sex again. He suddenly felt abandoned; he knew that these were Judas's kisses, absolving them of further duty to visit him ever again. This was the last time. Fuckers.

Then came a parade of his former alcoholic friends, some with beards, others bald, some fat, some thin, some smelling of tobacco, some of hay and dung and urine and sperm. His sense of smell increased and of sight decreased. And they all felt sorry for him, some even seemed to weep, but he got a sense that all of them also looked at his wife hungrily. She was sexy, fifteen years younger than him and most of them, and they were such lousy friends that they would probably paw her and fuck her on his deathbed. In the tone of her voice he sometimes thought he noticed some flirtation. And anyhow, they hadn't had sex in months, ever since Purim in Tel Aviv. In Jerusalem, they had forgotten about sex, so knocked out by heat and pilgrimage. Oh, he didn't even know it was the last time, and then, even when he was making love to her he wasn't quite with it, but imagining a nearly naked girl with torn stockings and thick red lips he'd seen in the streets of Tel Aviv.

His Czech cousins, ten years older than him, also came. One of them was a mechanical engineer who's spent ten years in Cuba, and who could never conduct a conversation without mentioning the wonders of Cuba. (Ever since Communism collapsed in Yugoslavia, the cousin could not go to Cuba on business anymore.) And sure enough, after going through the usual it's so sad spiel, he said, –When we landed in Havana... Davor didn't want to hear the rest. He wanted to be asleep, wanted this man to be gone out of his life, and for himself to be gone out of his life. Good thing morphine worked.

And then his sister visited from Sweden. She'd worked as a nurse there, but now, because of back-pains, was semi-retired. She loved to talk about death and tragedy, and he had a sense that she kind of enjoyed it, as long as it was the others and not herself who were dying.

His sister and his wife talked for a long time, while he writhed in pain. He asked for morphine, but who knows what came out of his mouth. Maybe he asked for fuck. He could not count on words coming out in the right order, and he couldn't count on his thoughts going on and making sense. There was silence. He couldn't hear them. Maybe he shrieked, he didn't know. He felt chilly, and the pain that amassed in his head and bones and abdomen was sharp and fiery; he'd eaten flames which couldn't be put out. His head hurt as though a primitive barber and dentist were cutting off his frontal lobe, and for all he knew, maybe that was happening, maybe someone was performing surgery to tranquilized or to remove part of his brain, the amygdala at least. And maybe his cancer had already eaten the amygdala, or had instead made it grow like a pear. The pain and the pressure in his brain were such that he grabbed his head with his hands and sat up.

–Oh, he's better, said his sister. Look, he has some strength. He's risen.

–Praise the Lord, said his wife. He has risen!

He saw the women clearly and felt lucid, and could hear and smell everything again, but he could not get rid of the pain or reach the pain. His half-blonde half-gray sister with thick framed glasses, which magnified her eyes, stared at him like a horned owl on an oak tree, such as he remembered in his early childhood, which had terrified him.

–Is there any more morphine? Davor asked with startling clarity.

–You've had your dose for the evening, said Alana.

–Oh really? Give me more, I am in pain.

–We'll have to get some more in the morning, you are out.

–Out?

–Yeah, just sleep till the morning, we'll get you plenty.

—It's easy for you to say that, he said.

—Look how clearly he speaks, he is better, said the Owl.

—You shut up, you old Owl, he said to his sister.

—Maybe he is not better, Alana said.

—Will you stop this bullshit, he said. All this pity and all, and I don't even have a decent pain killer. I'll show you what pain is, you sorry sluts.

Davor jumped out of bed, grabbed a chair and smashed it on the floor. It was an old chair, remaining from his grandfather's business. His grandfather had been a chair-maker in Pecs, Hungary, before he moved south, and he had died of stomach cancer. Sorry, Grand-Pa, he said, and smashed the leg stick remaining in his hand, over the earthenware flowerpot, which cracked.

His sister shrieked.

—Just you shriek, he said and punched her in the face so hard that she flew to the floor. Now that will teach you to feel sorry for me. What gives you the right, you smug Owl?

—Don't be like that, what did she do to you? She loves you, said Alana.

—Fuck love like this. I am tired of all the sympathy, you bunch of hypocrites. I am tired of all your Schadenfreude. You actually love it that I am dying, you'll inherit this whole bloody house, and it's soulful and exciting to watch someone die, isn't it. And now you are even close to Jesus. Which one? The one from the golden pink-marble tomb or the one from the plain limestone tomb?

He kicked Alana and then hit her too, bleeding her eye.

He chased the two women around the house, and in the middle of the chase, he attained a sense of well-being and near ecstasy. His pain was gone, and all his senses were as sharp as ever, he was young and strong, and he loved listening to them scream. It was like the best orgasmic pleasure screams he'd heard in best love making. Their screams proved that he was young and strong and in control. He wouldn't do it for long but just a few more minutes. It was better than lying and dying. This was life.

They locked themselves in the closet and called the ambulance. Two nurses, both male, came in, and Davor shouted at them, —I know what brings you here. You want to whore around with these two sluts.

The nurses tried to subdue him, but he punched one of them in the face. Now they called the cops, while Davor flipped tables, kicked in the TV screen. He picked up the TV and tossed it through the glass window into the street.

The police hit him over the head with a billy club.

—Wait a minute, that's not cool, Alana said. —He has brain cancer, and he's had strokes.

—Sorry, how else to calm him down? Shoot him? Or you want to leave him alone till he kills you?

The cops handcuffed Davor and placed him in the ambulance, drove him to the hospital in Slavonski Brod. There, he was heavily medicated and he passed out into fluffy dreams.

Alana and his sister visited, and played for him old Gospel music. The two of them sang:

> Amazing Grace, how sweet the sound,
> That saved a wretch like me....
> I once was lost but now am found,
> Was blind, but now, I see.

They all had tears in their eyes, and he smiled blissfully, or so he thought. He knew he was losing his brain, and the vague sounds from his past still didn't resurrect Christ for him. Christ had many graves, two in Israel, and thousands everywhere, and he would stay in the ground for more than three days, maybe three-thousand years. Davor still thought about Christ the man and didn't believe in the God. And then, he thought, what do I know? And what difference does it make whether I know something or don't, whether I believe or not. Should I be saved based on my opinions, and my opinion is that there's no God and no salvation, and if there's God, should he care about my opinion one way or another? If this is all his creating, even not believing in him is a form of celebrating him. And then, who needs celebrations? I've kind of celebrated, and it's embarrassing; I am sorry I inflicted pain on the ones who love me. I didn't think they loved me, but look, they've forgiven me everything, and they are playing this lame music from my childhood, ditties about love and God. It is touching, and I wish I could talk, but I can't open my mouth, can't lift my hand, I am done for, I am surprised I can think, if this is thinking. And look, their tears are falling onto me. Well, I can't cry and weep, what would be the point, and what's the point of asking for points. It's all over.

He thought he heard a doctor say, We can't do anything for him anymore. We have plenty of morphine for him, and you can take him home. He's all yours. There's nothing more we can do for him.

And two male nurses and two women in his life, wife and sister, took him home, where he lay for three days and three nights, and then died, with a mysterious half-smile on his thin blue lips, and his blue eyes pale, like the spring sky, irises only, with tiny and hazed-over pupils, reduced to milky black dots transitioning into the blue.

THE CONTRIBUTORS

DEREK NIKITAS is the Edgar Award-nominated author of the novels *Pyres* and *The Long Division* (St. Martin's Press) and *Extra Life* (Polis Books). Recently, he's co-written several novellas with bestselling author James Patterson, including *Diary of a Succubus*. His short fiction has been published in *The Ontario Review, Five Points, Chelsea, New South, Ellery Queen Mystery Magazine, Thuglit,* and elsewhere. With an MFA from UNC-Wilmington and a PhD from Georgia State University, he teaches fiction writing at the University of Rhode Island and lives not far from Lovecraft's old haunts.

JESSICA ANTHONY is the author of the novel *The Convalescent* (McSweeney's/Grove) and *Chopsticks* (Penguin/Razorbill), a multimedia novel created in collaboration with designer Rodrigo Corral. Anthony's short stories can be found in *Best New American Voices, Best American Nonrequired Reading, McSweeney's, The Idaho Review, Cutbank* and elsewhere. She has recently received fellowships from the Creative Capital Foundation for Innovative Literature, the Bogliasco Foundation and the Maine Arts Commission. Anthony is spending the summer of 2017 working on her next book while guarding the Mária Valéria Bridge between Ezstergom, Hungary, and Štúrovo, Slovakia. She lives in Portland, Maine.

JASON OCKERT is the author of Wasp Box, a novel, and two collections of short stories: Neighbors of Nothing and Rabbit Punches. Winner of the Dzanc Short Story Collection Contest, the Atlantic Monthly Fiction Contest, and the Mary Roberts Rinehart Award, he was also a finalist for the Shirley Jackson Award and the Million Writers Award. His work has appeared in journals and anthologies including *Best American Mystery Stories*, *Oxford American*, *One Story*, and *McSweeney's*.

BRIAN EVENSON is the author of a dozen books of fiction, most recently the story collection *A Collapse of Horses* and the novella *The Warren*. His books *Windeye* and *Immobility* were both finalists for a Shirley Jackson Award. His novel *Last Days* won the American Library Association›s award for Best Horror Novel of 2009. His novel *The Open Curtain* was a finalist for an Edgar Award and an International Horror Guild Award. He is the recipient of three O. Henry Prizes as well as an NEA fellowship. He lives in Los Angeles and teaches in the School of Critical Studies at CalArts.

JOE OESTREICH is the author of three books of creative nonfiction: *Partisans* (2017), *Lines of Scrimmage* (co-written with Scott Pleasant, 2015), and *Hitless Wonder* (2012). He teaches at Coastal Carolina University in Conway, SC. "Tricoter" sprang from a conversation Joe and his wife Kate once had, a dialogue that struck Joe as Hills-Like-White-Elephants-esque because of the oblique way he and Kate were talking about whether to have a baby. That the exchange happened on Paris's Left Bank, site of Hemingway's movable feast, was a fortunate coincidence.

STEFAN KIESBYE is the author of *Next Door Lived a Girl, Your House is on Fire, Your Children All Gone, Fluchtpunkt Los Angeles, The Staked Plains,* and *Knives, Forks, Scissors, Flames.* He teaches creative writing at Sonoma State University.

STACY BIERLEIN is the author of the story collection *A Vacation on the Island of Ex-Boyfriends* and a co-editor of the short fiction anthology *Men Undressed: Women Writers and the Male Sexual Experience.* Her award-winning anthology of international fiction, *A Stranger Among Us: Stories of Cross Cultural Collision and Connection,* is used in university classrooms across the country. In 1997 she had the honor to participate in Grace Paley's summer fiction workshop at the Fine Arts Work Center in Provincetown.

JANE DYKEMA'S work has appeared in *Big Big Wednesday, Cosmonauts Avenue, Volt,* and elsewhere. She's a Massachusetts Cultural Council Fellow and holds an MFA from UMass Amherst. She teaches writing at Clark University and Grub Street. "There's no way to cover ZZ Packer's "Brownies," for me, except very broadly to honor the premise of kids operating under a misunderstanding, the tangential discovery of some disappointing adult truths, and a narrator who is a thoughtful accessory to the main action. Race plays a role in the story I wrote in that a Puerto Rican character uses white characters' racist assumptions to protect something he loves, and in doing so, unintentionally motivates the kids into action."

ALEXANDER LUMANS was the Spring 2014 Philip Roth Resident at Bucknell University. His fiction has appeared in *Gulf Coast, TriQuarterly, Story Quarterly,* and *Black Warrior Review,* among others. "As a lifelong fan of O'Connor, the trick was deciding which story to cover. I wanted to take a contemporary technological spin on her work, so when I remembered the deaf, voiceless Lucynell, I realized I had a voice that still needed to be heard. After years of reading Craigslist Missed Connections posts, I loved pairing Lucynell's thoughts with a medium that asks for random chance to be the crucible for future love (or a doomed honeymoon)."

BROCK CLARKE is the author of six books of fiction, most recently the novels *The Happiest People in the World*, *Exley* (which was a Kirkus Book of the Year and finalist for the Maine Book Award), and *An Arsonist's Guide to Writers' Homes in New England* (which was a national bestseller, an American Library Associate Notable Book of the Year, a #1 Book Sense Pick, a Borders Original Voices in Fiction selection, and a *New York Times Book Review* Editor's Choice pick). His books have been reprinted in a dozen international editions, and have been awarded the Mary McCarthy Prize for Fiction, the Prairie Schooner Book Series Prize, a National Endowment for Arts Fellowship, and an Ohio Council for the Arts Fellowship, among others. He lives in Portland and teaches creative writing at Bowdoin College.

TERESE SVOBODA is the author of six books of fiction, seven books of poetry, a memoir, a biography, and a book of translation from a South Sudanese language. She has won a Guggenheim, the Bobst Prize in fiction, the Iowa Prize for poetry, an NEH grant for translation, and the O. Henry Award for the short story. A three-time winner of the New York Foundation for the Arts fellowship, she has also received the Graywolf Nonfiction Prize, a Pushcart Prize for the essay, a Bellagio Fellowship for a libretto, and the Jerome Foundation Award in video.

JEFF PARKER is the author of several books including *Where Bears Roam the Streets: A Russia Journal, Ovenman,* and *The Taste of Penny.* He teaches fiction writing in the UMass MFA.

JANE RIDGEWAY was born and raised in the Pacific Northwest, and received her MFA in Creative Writing from the University of Oregon in 2015. She is a teacher and journalist living in Silicon Valley.

TIBOR FISCHER was born in Stockport in 1959, the son of Hungarian refugees His first novel, *Under the Frog* was shortlisted for the Booker Prize in 1993. He is the author of four other novels, *The Thought Gang, The Collector Collector, Voyage to the End of the Room* and *Good to be God* as well as a collection of short stories *Don't Read This Book If You're Stupid.* A Fellow of the Royal Society of Literature, his work has been published in twenty-five languages.

PAUL ELWORK is a writer, editor, and teacher living in New Jersey with his wife and four sons, not far from his hometown of Philadelphia. His fiction has appeared in *SmokeLong Quarterly, Philadelphia Stories, Word Riot,* and other journals. His novel, *The Girl Who Would Speak for the Dead,* was released in hardcover by Amy Einhorn Books and in paperback by Berkley Books.

JOSIP NOVAKOVICH teaches at Concordia University in Montreal. He has just published several short story collections, three essay collections, and a novel, *April Fool's Day.* His work has appeared in many journals and anthologies—*Ploughshares, The Paris Review,* the Pushcart Prize, The O. Henry Awards. "When the Saints Come" will also appear in his new collection, *The Heritage of Smoke.*

ORIGINAL STORIES

H.P. LOVECRAFT, "Cthulhu." Possible influences on Lovecrafts's 1928 short story include Tennyson's "The Kraken" and Scott-Elliot's "The Story of Atlantis."

EDGAR ALLEN POE, "The Tell-Tale Heart." *The Pioneer* released the story in 1843. It originally began with an epigraph quoting Henry Wadsworth Longfellow's poem, "A Psalm of Life."

SHIRLEY JACKSON, "The Lottery." Published in *The New Yorker* in 1948, "The Lottery" generated more mai—and its fair share of cancellations—than any other work of fiction the magazine had ever printed.

RAYMOND CARVER, "The Neighbors." *Esquire Magazine* published "The Neighbors" in 1971. It was later included in Carver's collection *Will You Please Be Quiet, Please?.*

ERNEST HEMINGWAY, "Hills Like White Elephants." The story first appeared in *Transition* in 1927 and later that year in the collection *Men Without Women.*

JACK LONDON, "To Build a Fire." First printed in 1902, it is the darker 1908 version of "To Build a Fire" that has survived.

GRACE PALEY, "Wants." "Wants" is the opening story of Paley's 1974 collection, *Enormous Changes at the Last Moment.*

ZZ PACKER, "Brownies." Published in Packer's 2003 collection *Drinking Coffee Elsewhere*, "Brownies" has been widely anthologized.

FLANNERY O'CONNOR, "The Life You Save May Be Your Own." O'Connor included this short story in *A Good Man Is Hard to Find*, released in 1955.

JOHN CHEEVER, "Reunion." *The New Yorker* published "Reunion" in 1962.

DONALD BARTHELME, *The Dead Father*. Barthelme's post-modernist novel was published in 1975 by Farrar, Straus and Giroux.

NIKOLAI GOGOL, "The Nose." Gogol's satire was first printed in Alexander Pushkin's literary magazine *The Contemporary*, in 1836.

ISAAC BABEL, "My First Goose." "My First Goose" appeared in *Red Calvary*, Babel's collection of short stories chronicling the Soviet-Polish war of 1920.

HOMER, *The Iliad*. One of the oldest recorded stories in human history, *The Iliad* was written in Greece around 750 B.C.

NATHANIEL HAWTHORNE, "Young Goodman Brown." Like much of Hawthorne's work, this tale is set in 17th century Puritan New England. It was originally printed in 1835 in *The New England Magazine*.

LEO TOLSTOY, *The Death of Ivan Ilyich*. His 1886 novella is widely considered a masterpiece of Tolstoy's late fiction.

ACKNOWLEDGMENTS

I would like to thank Alli Geissel, Olivia Keogh, Deborah Lightcap, and Sean Johnson for their work on this anthology, their dedication and unwavering enthusiasm.

I also want to thank Gillian Conoley and *Volt Magazine*, Noelle Oxenhandler, Ianthe Brautigan Swensen, and the English department at Sonoma State University.

Special thanks to Dean Thaine Stearns for his vision and support.

And thanks to all the authors who answered my emails; Sanaz Kiesbye, Barbara Frohlech, Sandra Piantanida, Linda Eichhorn, and Tai Russotti, who helped me every step of the way.

CPSIA information can be obtained
at www.ICGtesting.com
Printed in the USA
FSOW02n2350080417
32829FS